BOOKS BY KRISTI HOLL

Just Like a Real Family
Mystery by Mail
Footprints Up My Back
The Rose Beyond the Wall
First Things First

First
Things
First

First Things First

Kristi D. Holl

Atheneum 1986 New York

Library of Congress Cataloging-in-Publication Data

Holl, Kristi D.
First things first.

Summary: To earn money for camp, Shelley opens a
portable garage sale and becomes so successful that to
find time for the rest of her life, she has to learn to
put first things first.
[1. Moneymaking projects—Fiction. 2. Business
enterprises—Fiction] I. Title.
PZ7.H7079Fi 1986   [Fic]   85-22941
ISBN 0-689-31201-6

Published simultaneously in Canada by
Collier Macmillan Canada, Inc.
Composition by Heritage Printers, Inc.,
Charlotte, North Carolina
Printed and bound by Fairfield Graphics
Fairfield, Pennsylvania
Designed by Christine Kettner
First Edition

To
RANDY,
MATT,
JENNY,
LAURIE
and
JACQUI--
who help me keep
first things first

Contents

First
Things
First

1  Up in Smoke

SHELLEY GORDON finished shaving the third red crayon, then piled the pieces into a small heap. "Isn't this enough *yet?*" she asked.

"Probably." Anna slowly stirred the hot wax. "Drop the shavings in here a few at a time."

Shelley sprinkled the red crayon pieces into the hot wax. A minute later Anna poured the cherry-red wax into molds she'd made from eggshells cut in half.

"What about wicks?" Shelley asked, trying to hurry her best friend.

"I'll use those short stiff wicks from the hobby shop." Anna flipped her black waist-length hair over her shoulder.

Ever since camp last summer, when they'd learned candlemaking, Anna had gone crazy making her own.

She filled seashells, old dishes, and now eggshells with wax. Anna's bedroom resembled an overstocked candle shop.

Shelley hooked her size-nine jogging shoes around the kitchen stool's legs. "Hey, have you registered for camp yet? Let's sign up together."

"There's still seven weeks till the deadline." Anna leaned on her elbows. "Just think—our fourth year at Forest Lake."

"*Finally* we'll be out of the baby group. Last year all the neat stuff happened in the junior high cabin. Remember when those three girls dragged sleeping bags up on the cabin roof?"

"And remember all their screeching when that bat flew over?" Anna filled the last eggshell.

"That was neat! Then our counselors tore outside when somebody yelled a skunk was under their blanket!"

"*Somebody?* That was you!"

Shelley grinned, then stretched. "Hooray for Fridays! You doing anything this weekend?"

"I'm going to some garage sales tomorrow." Anna pierced the last shellful of wax with a wick. "I'm hunting matching glass cups and saucers to use for candle holders."

"I don't know what I'm going to do, but if I don't get home for supper, I'll be grounded." Shelley grabbed her sixth-grade math book from the counter. "Call you tomorrow."

She jogged the eight blocks home in less than

three minutes. Although she tripped over her feet at school all the time, Shelley loved running. It made her feel coordinated, almost graceful.

Turning up the curved driveway, Shelley glanced at the maple canopy of shade overhead. She loved where they lived, from the dusty tire swing to the sagging hammock strung between two oaks. At the side door, Shelley caught a movement in the backyard. She switched direction and headed toward the vegetable garden.

"Hi, Dad!" Shelley tossed her math book on the grass. "What are you planting?"

"A new kind of peas—sugar snap. You eat shells and all." Her dad straightened after covering a row of seeds.

He hiked his baggy jeans up and tucked in his plaid workshirt. Shelley grinned. She'd inherited her thinness from her dad, but unlike him, she could usually find a belt to keep her pants up.

Shelley picked up two stakes tied together with a long piece of twine. "Let me help." She pushed one stake into the freshly tilled earth, then stretched the twine across the garden.

"Thanks, honey." Shelley's dad hoed a furrow down the length of the twine. "Where'd you go after school?"

"Anna's. She made more candles." Shelley ripped open the sugar snap package. "This is about the zillionth time since we learned how in camp last year."

"That reminds me," her dad said, leaning on the

hoe handle. "You've gone to Forest Lake for four years—"

"And this year'll be the best! We graduate to the junior high cabin." Shelley poked pea seeds an inch apart into the furrow. "Camp's the best part of summer. The deadline to register is over a month away, but I told Anna we should sign up right away."

"I'm afraid you can't." Mr. Gordon pushed back his sandy hair, leaving a muddy streak across his forehead. "I'm sorry, Shelley, but there's no money to send you to Forest Lake this year."

Shelley dropped her handful of seeds. "But *why?*"

"We got a letter. Camp went up to forty-five dollars this year. I just don't see how we can spare the money." He stooped to pick up the spilled seeds. "There were unusual expenses this year."

"You mean the furnace?" Last winter, during a sub-zero January blizzard, their ancient oil-burner had quit for good. The repairman told them the broken part they needed wasn't even being manufactured anymore.

Shelley's dad covered the seeds, then patted down the dirt. "We'll be paying on the furnace loan for another six months. And then, Missy was so sick."

Shelley crumbled a small dirt clod between her fingers. Now that her dad mentioned it, she remembered overhearing her parents' voices late at night. They'd whispered about the new furnace and hospital bills eating up their meager savings. Shelley sighed. She knew her dad was serious about missing camp.

He wiped his muddy hands on the grass. "I'm sorry. I know how you love Forest Lake. Right now, though, I don't know where the money would come from."

"I understand." Shelley swallowed hard, then picked up her math book and turned toward the house. "I'd better go help Mom with supper."

On the back steps, Shelley breathed deeply several times before opening the screen door. Even though her summer dreams had just gone up in smoke, she refused to let her mom see any tears. Squaring her shoulders, she stepped into the kitchen.

Just inside the door, Shelley did a quick hop over her six-month-old baby sister lying on the fringed rug. Picking her up, she rubbed the baby's stomach.

"Hi, Cassie." She balanced the baby on her hip. "Give Shelley a big smile?"

Cassie bopped Shelley on the nose with her hippopotamus teething ring. Drool ran down the baby's chin and dripped on her bib.

"Mom?" Shelley spotted her mother crouched under a decrepit wooden table. "What's that?"

"Isn't this the most marvelous table? Aunt Virginia brought this by today. It was just collecting dust in her shed, and she knew we'd need a bigger table soon." She caressed the chipped green paint.

Shelley studied the table up close. What a wreck. "Um, it's real nice."

Her mother chuckled and crawled out. "I know it doesn't look like much now. But when it's stripped down and the natural oak's varnished, it'll be gorgeous."

Shelley laid Cassie on the floor and tickled the bottoms of her feet. Giggling, the baby rolled over twice and bumped into the table. She gnawed greedily on the table leg.

"Pull her away from there, Shelley." Her mother reached into the refrigerator for a cold carrot stick. "I don't want her to swallow any old paint chips."

Shelley gave Cassie the carrot stick. "Mom? Dad said we can't afford the camp fee this year." She stared at the gold linoleum, hoping her mother would say there was some mistake.

Her mom sat Indian-style on the floor next to Shelley. "We hoped we'd find a way. If it hadn't been for Missy's pneumonia last month, we could have swung it."

"I know. It's just that—"

Before Shelley could finish, Missy careened around the corner of the kitchen and crashed her baby buggy into the wall. Raggedy Ann flew from the buggy, landing in the wastebasket.

"Melissa!" her mom cried. "Watch where you're going!" She inspected the new scratch on the wall. Slivers of plaster flaked off in her hand.

Missy shrugged and pushed back her red and white football helmet. "I can't help it. When Daddy's old football hat falls over my eyes, I splat into the walls."

"Just try to be more careful." Turning, their mother gasped and hurried to where the baby again slobbered on the table leg. "I'll be relieved when Cassie's new teeth finally come in." She rinsed off the carrot, made kissing noises at the baby, then changed Cassie's soggy bib.

Shelley sighed. It was like living in a zoo. An entire conversation without any interruptions was impossible these days.

Giving up, Shelley plodded down the hall. Disappointment washed over her as she trudged up the creaky stairs.

All year she and Anna had made detailed plans for their first year in the junior cabin. She might as well forget them now. No way could she earn forty-five dollars on her own in the next month.

Shelley decided to postpone breaking the awful news to Anna until Monday. Too depressed for anything more strenuous, she brooded in front of the TV that night until bedtime.

The alarm clock woke Shelley early the next morning: 6:20, its blinking digits read. Mourning doves cooed softly outside. Across the room, Missy's rhythmic snore was muffled by the tangled hair across her face.

Without warning Shelley's disappointment over camp engulfed her again. She'd hoped her chances would look better in the morning, but they didn't. No fairy godmother had waved her magic wand, turning her bottle cap collection into gold pieces.

Restless, Shelley crawled out of bed, then pulled on her shorts, T-shirt, leg warmers, jogging shoes, and headband. Holding her breath, she stepped over the hall floor boards that creaked, then crept past Cassie's nursery.

Ten seconds later she was down the carpeted stairs and outside. At the bottom of the driveway Shelley did a few stretches, then took off. Between the sidewalk and the street, she jogged on the spongy dew-soaked grass. Soon she was gasping. She'd covered six blocks before the squeezing sensation in her chest subsided. After gaining her second wind, her legs moved with a graceful rhythm all their own.

Shelley loved that feeling. At school she felt awkward and unsure of herself. But when she ran, it was so different. She covered the ground with easy strides. Teasing, her classmates had called her "Flash." With Gordon for a last name, the nickname stuck.

At a stoplight at Third and Westlake, she yanked up her leg warmers. So what if they were sleeves from a discarded sweater, with elastic sewn in the tops and bottoms. She still thought she looked like an ad right out of *Running Magazine*.

Shelley tucked some frizzy hair into her sweatband, then jogged across the street on a green light.

"Hey, Flash! Where's the fire?" yelled a voice from across the street.

Shelley pivoted. Nathan Atkins, a boy from her class, had his newspaper bag slung over his shoulder. She waved, wishing she could think of a clever remark to yell back. Two blocks later she'd think of something brilliant and witty. But, as usual, when she needed a quick answer, her brain was on hold.

Shelley crossed the street diagonally and headed back toward home. Thinking of Anna, her new-found energy drained right out her toes. With no Forest Lake camp, summer vacation just wouldn't be the same.

2 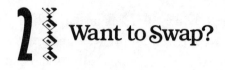 Want to Swap?

SHELLEY'S DAD claimed that a border of marigolds, or "stink weeds," as he called them, would keep bugs and rabbits out of a garden. Needing time to think that afternoon, Shelley carried the spade, bucket, and three packets of seeds out to the garden plot.

When the south border was nearly planted, she spotted their neighbor across the backyard. Holding large shears and a Mason jar, Mrs. Sutton studied her peony bushes.

"Hi, Mrs. Sutton." Shelley waved her hoe in the air.

"Shelley! Gorgeous day, isn't it?" Mrs. Sutton waddled over to the boundary of the two yards. "I'm going to cut some iris and peonies to take to the hospital this afternoon."

"Somebody sick?"

Mrs. Sutton's chin wobbled as she shook her head. "No, my niece had a baby girl last night!" She eyed the canning jar and frowned. "I guess I'll just tie a pink ribbon around the jar." Her shaggy gray eyebrows drew together.

"I can find you a pretty baby-girl planter."

"You can? Where?"

"In our basement. Mom had three girls—and got millions of flowers in pink pots." Shelley dropped her hoe. "I'll be right back. I know it'll be okay."

"Well, if you're sure, that would be lovely." Mrs. Sutton's tiny eyes squinted shut with pleasure. "With my pink peonies and white iris, I could make a beautiful bouquet."

Inside, Shelley found her mother under the dirty oak table, rubbing a smelly concoction onto the peeling wood. Dissolved green paint came off on a worn-out diaper rag.

Shelley crouched down by the table. "Mom, can I give Mrs. Sutton a baby-girl planter? She's taking some flowers to the hospital for her niece."

"Sure. The pots are in the tornado room, I think. You'll have to rummage around a little."

"I can find them."

Shelley clomped down the wooden basement stairs. When her face touched a cobweb, she wiped it away with the back of her hand. In the musty basement, she yanked on the string hanging in the center of the room. The swinging sixty-watt bulb cast dancing shadows as Shelley headed to the closed door at the far end of the basement.

She dragged the heavy door open. The screech it made as it scraped the cement floor set Shelley's teeth on edge.

Inside the six-foot by eight-foot tornado room, she groped for the second cord and with a pull, she turned on the light. Although really a storage cellar for potatoes and apples, it had been the "tornado room" since Shelley was three. During scary tornado warnings, the tiny cement-walled room was their storm cellar.

Shelley hadn't been in the room for months. Since then, junk had accumulated on the shelves lining the three walls.

She started on the bottom shelf and lifted the mildewed cardboard boxes to the floor. From the far corner, Shelley heard the *scritch-scratch* of scurrying mice. Shuddering, she bent over the boxes.

No baby planters were in the first boxes of old junk. She dug past a set of red picnic dishes, some metal curtain rods, a miniature set of wrenches, and a plastic bag of dirty costume jewelry.

Finally, in a wooden box, she found several ceramic planters. After choosing one shaped like a cradle, with a music box that still played "Rock-A-Bye, Baby," Shelley shoved the dusty boxes back onto the splintery shelves. Dust whirled, and she sneezed three times in rapid succession.

While hoisting the last box to the top shelf, a thought struck her. Through the gloom she stared at the discarded boxes of junk. Scrubbed up, some of it could be useable. If she cleaned it up herself, maybe her parents would let her hold a garage sale. With some real luck, she could raise enough money to go to Forest Lake after all!

Grabbing the cradle music box, Shelley kicked the storage room door closed. She raced upstairs, anxious to ask her mother about a garage sale.

But there was no chance. Mrs. Sutton sat in a dinette chair, a glass of lemonade in front of her. She bounced Cassie on her knees.

At the sink, Shelley scrubbed the cradle planter with a paper towel, then wound the music box. She placed it on the table near Mrs. Sutton. "Rock-A-Bye, Baby" drifted through the kitchen.

"How lovely!" Mrs. Sutton touched the planter with a stubby finger. "Sure you won't want to keep this?"

Shelley's mom reached for Cassie, who chewed on Mrs. Sutton's shirt sleeve. "You're welcome to the planter. You can only use so many pink pots."

"Thanks for going to all this trouble, Shelley. Janey will adore it." She waddled to the door and let herself out.

After Mrs. Sutton left, Shelley turned excitedly to her mom. "I found all kinds of neat stuff downstairs—"

"Oh, *great*." Her mother held Cassie away from her lap. The leg of her jeans showed a large wet spot. "Looks like somebody needs changing."

Shelley's mother started down the hall, then called over her shoulder. "By the way, Anna called while you were outside. She wants you to come over tonight after supper. Around seven-thirty."

"Okay." At the mention of Anna's name, Shelley's spirits drooped. As rotten as she already felt, she expected to feel worse after telling Anna about camp.

"I'll be in the garden if you need me," Shelley called.

She'd finished the south flower border when Mrs. Sutton jiggled across the backyard. In her pudgy hands was the cradle planter, holding pink and white flowers in a tight cluster. A pink ribbon added a professional-looking touch.

"Looks as good as a florist's, doesn't it?" Mrs. Sutton asked.

"It turned out pretty."

Mrs. Sutton pulled two dollar bills from her apron pocket. "I want to give you something for the work you did, finding the planter and cleaning it up."

"I can't take it. Anyway, it was Mom's planter." Shelley stuck her hands in her pockets.

"I figured you might say that. Then how about if I *trade* you something for the planter?"

She reached into her other pocket and brought out a small stained-glass clown figurine. Shelley recognized the sun-catcher from Mrs. Sutton's kitchen window.

The colorful glass sparkled. "Are you sure?"

"Absolutely." Mrs. Sutton pressed the glittering clown into Shelley's hand. "We'll call it an even trade, okay?"

The clown *would* look great in her bedroom's east window. "Okay," Shelley agreed. "It's a trade."

On the way to Anna's house that night, Shelley thought again about her garage sale idea. It could work, but what if her parents didn't want to part with the dirty junk in the basement? Even if they agreed to her plan, she'd have to sell a truckload of junk to raise forty-five dollars.

At Anna's house, Shelley took a deep breath and rang the bell. How could she tell her best friend that all their plans for the junior cabin were off?

Anna's mom invited her in. An ear-splitting screech from Anna's record player echoed down the hall. Shelley followed the noise, surprised to see Charlene Mason and Kendra Butler. Anna sat on the floor, painting her toenails.

"Feast your eyes on these!" Kendra swayed like a hula dancer, waving her fingers back and forth in Shelley's face.

Anna tossed her long braid over her shoulder and grinned. "Come on, Shell, you're next. What colors do you want—green with white glitter, or red with white polka dots?"

The floor was littered with albums. Shelley picked her way through them. It was impossible to think. Charlene's favorite rock star screamed from the record player.

Glitter sparkled on Charlene's green Dracula fingernails. "Beautiful, aren't they?"

"Mmm-mmm," Shelley mumbled. "I think I'll try red and white. Where'd you get these wild colors?"

Anna waved her nail file toward the row of small bottles. "I found them at Bergman's Drug Store. All I did was add a little glitter."

She proceeded to paint Shelley's fingernails a flashy fire-engine red. "Blow on your nails for a couple minutes. When they're dry, I'll put the white dots on them."

Charlene swayed around the bedroom, mouthing the words to the song on the record while she studied Anna's creations. "Where'd you get all the neat candles?" She held an antique Coke bottle filled with green wax.

"She makes them," Shelley said proudly.

Anna nodded. "I bought the Coke bottle and the china dishes at garage sales. I'm saving the dishes for a candle-making party I want to have. I only paid a dime for the bottle and around a quarter for the others."

Shelley's hopes took a nose dive. Were all garage sale items so cheap? She'd never raise enough money for camp at that rate, even if she hocked every single thing in her family's basement.

Kendra lay on her back on Anna's bed. Her head hung over the end. "Do you go to lots of garage sales?"

"Whenever I can," Anna said, "usually on Saturday mornings. You wouldn't believe the stuff for sale. Old Fifties records, jeans for a dollar, books, stuff to decorate your room. You name it."

Charlene whirled gracefully. "If you find any pearl or bead necklaces, could you buy them for me? I'd pay you. I'm making a new beach bag decorated with old beads. I imagine it'll start a new trend." Charlene always thought she was going to start a new trend.

Kendra flipped over backwards and landed on the floor. "I have piano lessons on Saturday morning, or I'd go with you to some garage sales." She wandered around the room, studying Anna's posters of kittens and bears.

"Did you want anything special?" Anna asked.

"I collect elephants—little figurines or stuffed ones. If you saw some, could you buy them for me? I'd trade you for some posters I have at home."

"Maybe. I'll keep my eyes open," Anna promised. "Come here, Shelley. Let me add those white polka dots." She sprinkled globby white spots on Shelley's red fingernails.

While blowing on her white speckles, Shelley mulled over Kendra's and Charlene's words. They both wanted to buy or trade for special things, just like Mrs. Sutton had traded her sun-catcher for the baby planter.

Shelley sat forward suddenly, smearing the white dots on two fingernails.

Maybe there was an idea here. A garage sale alone might not make enough money, but what about swapping? For a commission, she could hunt at garage sales for things her friends wanted to collect.

She continued to blow on her nails in silence. Maybe, just *maybe*, she'd go to Forest Lake camp yet.

3 ❖ In Business

ON SUNDAY afternoon, Shelley descended again to the dark tornado room. Her mom had said it was okay to sort through the boxes for things to sell.

The first box she poked through contained a plastic shower curtain, shower rods, three yellow ceramic fish and leftover tiles from when her dad had remodeled the bathroom.

Under the tile, she discovered a hand mirror, streaked but in good condition. A unicorn was painted on the back, its tail twisting down the mirror handle. Whistling, Shelley placed her treasure in the large shoebox she'd brought downstairs.

Her first piece of merchandise. She was in business!

It took four hours to paw through the rest of the

boxes. At six-thirty, she sat back on her heels and wiped her sweaty face. Her arms and back ached, but it'd been worth her time.

Besides the mirror, she'd found a purse-sized photo album, an elephant-shaped key chain, a pocket knife with a deer carved into the handle, and a beaded purse missing a lot of beads. In addition, there was a pen shaped like a long ear of corn, a bean bag frog, and an owl figurine.

She couldn't open a store yet, but it was a start.

The beaded bag was intended for Charlene. The shiny beads could be removed and sewn onto her beach bag. Since Kendra wanted elephant-shaped things, the key chain would be perfect for her.

Upstairs, Shelley wolfed down three Fig Newtons while Mrs. Gordon sorted through the shoebox. "I'd forgotten most of this junk was downstairs. There's nothing here I want." She piled everything back into the box. "You're welcome to try to sell this stuff."

"Thanks, Mom."

Shelley knew she'd be lucky to raise even half the money she needed. But if she could make twenty or twenty-five dollars, she hoped her parents might somehow come up with the other half. It was worth a try.

In bed that night her hopes rode a roller coaster. They soared high, then slammed back down. One moment she was sure it'd be a cinch to raise the camp money. The next minute she was positive she'd never see Forest Lake Camp again as long as she lived.

Finally, exhausted, she dropped off, but overslept the next morning. Her bedside clock read 7:13.

Rats. She'd missed her morning run. Shelley untangled her long granny nightgown from around her legs and rolled over the side of the bed. She landed with a thud, whacking her crazy bone.

Jerked fully awake, she rubbed her elbow and gazed around the messy room. At the sight of her shoebox on the desk, she brightened. She'd nearly forgotten. Today she was going into business!

Shelley gobbled her blueberry pancakes and was out the back door fifteen minutes early. She hugged her blue shoebox close, her math book balanced on top.

When she arrived at school she spotted Charlene near the swings with Anna. Although her heart thudded under her T-shirt, Shelley tried to appear casual as she strolled toward them.

"Hi, everybody." Shelley sat cross-legged beside Anna. She pretended to wipe invisible dust from the lid of her shoebox.

"What's in there?" Charlene pointed with a glittering green fingernail. "Something for the science exhibit?"

"Not exactly." Shelley concentrated on retying her jogging shoe. "I found some things in our basement. I thought . . . That is, maybe there's something here you'd want. To buy, that is," she added in a small voice.

"Let me see." Charlene removed the lid. Without comment, she flicked from the small things on top to the larger items on the bottom. "Mostly junk."

"I'm sure it's as good as garage sale stuff," Shelley said stiffly. "You wouldn't want to buy the purse, would you? You *said* you needed beads for the beach bag you're making."

Charlene pulled it out of the box. "How much do you want for it?"

Shelley's heart hammered. She wanted to say a dollar, but wondered if it was too much. "I guess, well, I think seventy-five cents would be fair."

"Seventy-five cents? These beads are sewn on pretty tight. It would take forever to get them off." She poked around in her suede coin purse. "I have thirty-five cents. I'll pay that much."

Shelley chewed her bottom lip. Only thirty-five cents? That wasn't much. On the other hand, it was *something*. Maybe her friends deserved a cut rate.

Sighing, Shelley nodded. "Thirty-five's okay." She dropped the money in her jeans pocket.

Anna braided and rebraided her long hair. "What's with the portable garage sale?"

Shelley wished Charlene would leave. Instead, she inched even closer. Shelley took a deep breath. "Dad told me they can't afford to send me to Forest Lake this year."

"What? Why not? That can't be true!" Anna

grabbed Shelley's wrist. "We always go together!"

Shelley's stomach churned. "We had a lot of expenses this year. Remember when Missy was in the hospital? And when they replaced our old furnace?"

Anna nodded glumly. "I remember." Shelley's family had spent the day at Anna's during the blizzard while men installed their new furnace.

Shelley picked at her polka-dotted fingernails. "Forty-five dollars is too much this year. That's why I'm selling this stuff from our basement."

Charlene leaned forward. "Is this everything, or do you have more?"

"This is it."

Anna studied Shelley's shoebox of merchandise. "Is there any chance you'll make enough money? I won't go to camp without you."

"I don't know if I'll make any money or not, but there's no reason for both of us to miss camp."

Anna shook her head stubbornly.

Shelley brushed the grass from her hands. "There's Kendra. I'll be right back."

Half a block down the sidewalk she met Kendra, who smiled and waved. At least she should be easier to talk to, Shelley thought. Dressed in jeans and tennis shoes like everyone else, Kendra wasn't as snobby as Charlene, the trend-setter.

"Hi, Kendra. Got a minute?" Shelley spoke in a rush, before she lost her nerve.

"What's up?" Kendra peered in Shelley's open shoebox.

"I found something I thought maybe you'd like." Shelley handed her the key chain shaped into a plump, wrinkled gray elephant.

Kendra turned the key chain over several times. "Why would I be interested in this old thing?"

"You collect things in the shape of elephants! That's what you told Anna."

"I said I collected stuffed elephants and figurines. They sit around my room." Kendra dropped the key chain back into the box. "What else have you got in there?"

She squatted down on the sidewalk and sorted through Shelley's box. Without a word, she shrugged an apology and handed back the box.

"Thanks, anyway," Shelley muttered.

The morning dragged by. While Shelley diagrammed sentences, Anna's pinched face, seen across the room, was a constant reminder of camp. Although it wasn't her fault, Shelley felt she'd let Anna down.

When the lunch bell rang, Shelley jumped and knocked the shoebox to the floor, where it up-ended. Its contents clattered across the aisle.

Her face hot, Shelley dropped to her knees to scoop up her belongings. Two boys nearly stepped on her fingers as they raced to the cafeteria.

A pair of dingy oversized basketball shoes stopped beside Shelley. She ignored them, reaching under her desk for the key chain and pocket knife, which she dropped into the box.

"Hey, Flash! What's that?" The pair of shoes belonged to David Forest.

"Just some junk." Shelley wished David would leave. Enough people had belittled her merchandise already. "Nothing you'd be interested in."

"What did you just pick up?" David asked again. "Let me see it."

Shelley glanced up, surprised. He sounded serious. She held out the wrinkled elephant.

"Not that. This." David dug to the bottom of the box. "Where'd you get this pocket knife?" He ran a finger over the carved deer.

"From my dad. He doesn't want it anymore." With her knees trembling, she added, "All this stuff is for sale."

"Really? Do you have any more pocket knives?"

"No, just this one." Remembering the other half of her plan, she added, "At garage sales I could find other pocket knives for you."

"I'll think about it." David held out the knife. "How much are you asking?"

"Well, it's a pretty special knife. You know, the carved deer and all."

He frowned, turning the knife over and over. "I'm a little short. I couldn't pay more than two dollars."

Shelley blinked. *Two dollars?* She'd only planned to charge a dollar for it and would have settled for fifty cents. She swallowed and smiled.

"I guess two dollars would be okay."

"When I go home for lunch, I'll get the two bucks." David reluctantly handed over the knife. "You won't sell this to somebody else before I get back, will you?"

"No, not even if someone offers me a lot more money." Shelley figured the odds against that were astronomical, but David didn't need to know.

"Thanks." David's basketball shoes slapped the tiled floor as he hurried to the door. "I'll get the money now. That makes eight knives in my collection so far."

Shelley stowed her shoebox under her chair, then left to join Anna for spaghetti in the cafeteria. She couldn't believe it. Her second sale already! Two dollars and thirty-five cents was a long way from forty-five dollars, but it was a start.

Sales were slow during the week, with Shelley only selling two more things. Sandra Dix, who took millions of snapshots of her dog, Princess, bought the photo album. Shelley's teacher, Miss Walters, said the owl figurine would make a perfect paper weight.

The following Saturday morning, Shelley cut her running time short after she'd jogged just half a mile. Anna and her mom were picking her up at eight, and she wanted to be ready. Together they'd hit the garage sales early.

Browsing through smelly garages and wet back-yards that morning, Shelley was surprised at the variety of stuff for sale. At tag sales, as Anna's mother called them, there was something for everybody.

Shelley copied other customers and pawed hurriedly through the overloaded tables. In her purse was the money from her school sales that week—nearly four dollars—in case she ran across any bead necklaces, pocket knives, or stuffed elephants.

"Ready to go, Shelley?" Anna's mom called.

Shelley glanced up in confusion. She hadn't inspected even half the tables. "I'm coming!" She clutched her purse and pushed through the crowd.

During the next two and a half hours, they visited seven houses. Shelley discovered "garage" sales could be held anywhere—in a garage, on a front porch, on the sidewalk, or in a yard. She also learned to grab fast, before a pushy customer snatched her purchase right from under her nose.

After careful consideration, she spent fifty cents for a black-handled pocket knife for David. Two strands of fake pearls for Charlene cost a dime each. She hoped to sell them at a gigantic profit. In addition, she bought several small things to add to her shoebox.

During the following week Shelley's spirits got a boost. David bought the knife, for two-fifty this time. Sandra eagerly paid a dollar for the paperback book on photography. She promised to bring her newest photos of Princess to school. And Charlene bought the necklaces for thirty cents each.

On Friday Shelley spread out her money across

her bed, then slowly counted it. So far, it wasn't much.

However, she still had five weeks to earn a lot more. Forty more dollars was too much to make in that time, but hopefully she'd earn a big chunk of the camp fee. Then maybe her dad would pay the rest.

She scooped the money into her Mickey Mouse bank. Deep down, Shelley knew her chances of going to Forest Lake were still almost next to nothing. But she could hope.

4  South Seas

"Ooww!" Shelley cried, peering over the edge of the large cardboard box she carried.

"You okay?" Her mother turned from where she stirred baby cereal. "What happened?"

"Nothing. Just stubbed my toe on Cassie's baby swing." Shelley soothed the startled baby, then set Cassie in gentle motion again.

Glancing in the mirror over the desk, Shelley noticed the humid air had already caused her hair to kink up around her face. She stuck out her tongue at the curls, hating her wild frizzy look. "Bye, Mom. See you after school."

"What's the rush?"

"I have a couple things to sell before school starts."

Her mom lifted Cassie from the swing and tied a bib under her plump chin. "Good luck! By the way, was Missy awake when you came down?"

Before Shelley could answer, the squeaky screen door opened and slammed shut. Missy slid into the room, still in her floor-length pajamas.

Mrs. Gordon sighed. "Missy, please don't go outside in your PJ's. You're too old for that, don't you think?"

"Where are you going, Shell?" Missy asked, ignoring her mom's question.

"To school." Shelley inched around her sister. "I have to be there early today."

"What about Corduroy? He's hungry." Missy planted herself squarely in the doorway. "You haven't fed him for days."

Shelley chewed her bottom lip. How could she have forgotten her own dog? Usually she stopped and played with her brown cocker spaniel right after she jogged in the morning. Then Shelley would feed and water him before going in for breakfast.

"Missy, could you feed him this morning?" Shelley glanced at the clock. "I won't forget again."

"Okay." Missy scratched her stomach. "Anyway, I *do* like feeding Corduroy. He jumps up and kisses me when we play."

"Thanks. Have fun at kindergarten this afternoon." Shelley ruffled Missy's hair. "See you tonight."

Juggling her cardboard box and books, Shelley hurried to school. She found Kendra in the rest room and sold her a stuffed elephant. Then David bought a knife before recess.

Nathan Atkins was with David when he bought the knife. Nathan offered to trade his new *1001 Spooky Riddles* book for a bag of small soldiers in her box. Shelley agreed, figuring she could get seventy-five cents for the book. The soldiers had only cost a quarter.

Adding quickly, Shelley realized she'd saved over twelve dollars so far. Of course that was still a million miles from forty-five dollars, but it was a start.

On the way back to her desk, Lisa Sargent and Jon Kruger stopped her. Lisa and Jon were the most popular kids in her class. Lisa, with her matching dimples and mascara-ed eyelashes, made Shelley nervous. And Jon—Shelley'd had a crush on him since third grade. Around him, she was either tongue-tied or she babbled.

Lisa stood poised like a ballerina, while Jon lounged on the corner of Shelley's desk. Jon's slow smile made Shelley's heart thump wildly. Although she'd had a long drink at the water fountain, her mouth felt dry as cotton balls.

Lisa batted her dark black eyelashes. "We need a favor. David says you find him knives at garage sales. We need something too."

Jon shook his long hair back off his forehead, but it dropped into place again over his left eye. "We're in charge of decorations for the band party next week."

Lisa interrupted smoothly. "The theme of the party is the South Seas—"

"And get this. We have to turn the gym into an *island*."

"South Seas?" Shelley stared blankly.

"Exactly." Lisa spoke crisply. "We'll put things on the walls—construction paper palm trees, blue waves, that kind of thing. But we need table and floor decorations."

Shelley pried her dry lips from her teeth. "Like seashells or something?"

"Good idea." Jon smiled slowly, his perfectly even white teeth right out of a toothpaste commercial. "Could you find us ten dollars' worth of decorations?"

Shelley tore her gaze away from Jon's perfect tan. "I'll try . . . this weekend."

"Great." Jon leaned over her desk. "We appreciate this, Shelley."

Shelley blinked rapidly, her mouth open. The final bell rang before she could think of a clever answer. "Why am I such a dope?" she mumbled as she watched Jon walk away. "Who knows how many years it will be before Jon Kruger sits on my desk again?"

That weekend Shelley haunted the garage sales listed in the newspaper. She biked across town twice, carrying her purchases home in the white wicker bike basket. To sales closer by, she dragged Missy's wagon. Pulling a little red wagon took a long time and made her feel ridiculous, but it was easier to cart things home that way.

By Saturday afternoon, she was exhausted. But she'd finally struck gold in her search for South Seas decorations.

At each sale, Shelley'd hunted first through the items on display. Then, before leaving, she showed each seller a written list of things she was looking for, asking if they had any items on her list they would sell.

Three different times, people had searched attics or basements for her. By the end of the morning, she'd found nearly everything on the list she and Anna had made Friday night.

On Monday morning, her dad offered to drive her to school. "You sure worked hard this weekend, Honey. We hardly saw you." He shifted her box and grocery sack. "Just don't overdo this swapping and selling."

"I *am* tired," Shelley admitted, slouched in the front seat, "but it was worth it. These island decorations only cost me four dollars, leaving six dollars profit."

Her dad raised his voice over the blaring radio. "I'm sorry you have to do this. I wish we had enough money to send you to Forest Lake."

Shelley glanced up in surprise. "It's not so bad. I *do* wish I were better at making people want to buy stuff, though."

Her dad ruffled her flyaway hair. "You've already made more from this venture than I dreamed you would. Who knows? You might make it to camp yet."

Shelley pushed back her hair and beamed.

Ten minutes later, Shelley waited in front of the school. When Lisa and Jon arrived, she nervously laid the South Seas decorations, one by one, on the sidewalk for them to examine.

The grocery sack held white and pink seashells, some shaped like clams, others spiraled. Two heavy pink conch shells were large enough for floor decorations.

Flustered by Jon watching her, Shelley held out an off-white clam shell. "These would make nice table decorations."

"Umm," was all Lisa said.

From the bottom of the sack, Shelley pulled a fish net smelling of seaweed. "This could be draped on a wall, with the driftwood I found under it." She held her breath, wishing Jon would say something.

Lisa reached into the box. "Look at this!" She lifted out a coconut with a pirate's face carved into it. A red bandana and eye patch completed the face. "This is perfect for the main refreshment table."

Shelley's voice squeaked. "At one place I told the seller about the South Seas decorations. He sold me those two big conch shells, plus this coconut head. Those three things cost more money than everything else combined."

"Good thing you mentioned money." Jon pulled

a crumpled ten-dollar bill from his back pocket. "I'd say we got our money's worth."

"I agree." Lisa helped Shelley repack the shells. "These are the best party decorations the band's ever had."

Lisa and Jon carried the box and sack inside to the band room. Shelley leaned against the building, staring at the ten-dollar bill. Now that Jon was gone and she could breathe again, she felt a surging sense of achievement.

Two days later as Shelley headed to the cafeteria, Anna darted out of the principal's office. Grinning, she grabbed Shelley's arm, waving a copy of the school paper in her face.

"Hey, Celebrity! Wait till you see this!" She folded the paper open to the second page. "I just bought it, hot off the presses. Here, read."

Dazed, Shelley skimmed the story. She couldn't believe it. The story in the school paper was about *her*. "Portable Garage Sale," the title said, by David Forest.

David had interviewed several kids in their class. There were comments from Kendra and Sandra, plus praise from Jon and Lisa about the party decorations. "She did a great job," Jon was quoted as saying.

Shelley reread Jon's words four times. She thought she was going to faint. Jon Kruger, the cutest boy in the sixth grade, had paid her a compliment! It was right there *in print*. The whole school could read it.

After lunch she was bombarded by questions as she walked into her classroom. "Hey, Flash, where's your portable garage?" "How much did you pay David to write that story?" "What's for sale, Flash?" "Hey, anybody know that famous person over there?"

Flustered, Shelley pretended not to hear. Being the center of attention wasn't as much fun as she'd thought it would be.

That entire afternoon Shelley heard Miss Walters through a thick fog. Jon's wonderful quote from the newspaper went round and round in her head. She kept her eyes lowered, afraid Jon might look at her. If he did, she knew she'd die.

At the end of English period, however, Miss Walters's announcement broke through her fog.

" . . . and rather than daily English papers," Miss Walters said, adjusting her pink-framed glasses, "I want each of you to do a three-week book project." Shelley leaned forward; she loved to read, so this sounded like fun. "Each student will read three books by a single author of his or her choice."

"Three!" came a hoarse whisper from the back of the room.

Miss Walters's words whistled through the wide gap between her two front teeth. "Take notes on these books as you read. Then, in a two-page report, compare the characters, plots and themes of the books." Her head bobbed, shaking her chopped-off straight hair.

Nathan waved his hand like a windmill. "How long do these books have to be?"

"The books must have chapters. However, the length is up to you, boys and girls." With her lispy whistle, her words came out "boyth and girlth."

Shelley nodded, already sure which author she'd choose. After school Shelley and Anna stopped uptown at the public library. For half an hour Shelley browsed, then chose two books by Doris Gates: *Sarah's Idea* and *Sensible Kate*.

Blue Willow, her third book for the project, was at home. It was an old book, and it had belonged to her mother. Shelley was already halfway through the story and loved it. She hoped she'd like the other two books just as much.

At home Shelley stacked the books on her nightstand, eager to begin her project right away. But by the time she got back upstairs that night, it was time for bed. It had taken the whole evening to clean up her new merchandise to take to school the next morning.

Shelley crawled under the covers and aimed her reading light at the fourth chapter of *Blue Willow*. However, after covering three pages, she couldn't remember anything she'd just read.

Yawning loudly, she started over.

Her head wobbled tiredly, so she scrunched down and lay back on her pillow. With the book three inches from her face, the words soon blurred together.

Finally, giving up, Shelley snapped off the light. She promised herself to begin the book project the very next night.

But right after supper the next night Missy crashed her mini-wheel and mashed her face into the sidewalk. With her mouth cut, three teeth loosened, and the skin scraped from her nose, her parents rushed her to the hospital emergency room for stitches.

While they were gone, Shelley watched Cassie. After her parents and Missy returned, Shelley went upstairs to review for her civics test. She detested that subject, but to pass sixth grade, each student was required to take nine weeks of classes on United States government.

Armed with a bag of red licorice, Shelley paced around her bedroom for twenty minutes, mumbling about senators and representatives.

When she finished, it was too late to do anything but sleep. But why worry? She was already into the fourth chapter of *Blue Willow*. With the weekend coming up, she'd finish that book and begin *Sensible Kate*.

Friday afternoon after school, Shelley found Missy sprawled on the back step, feeding Corduroy some puppy biscuits. With a little stab of guilt, Shelley realized she hadn't fed her dog since Tuesday or Wednesday.

She joined Missy on the step. "How's your face?" she asked. Corduroy wiggled over to Shelley's lap and licked her chin.

"Okay, I guess," Missy mumbled, barely moving her scabbed lips.

"Mom said the cuts should heal without any scars." Shelley casually scratched her dog behind his brown floppy ears. "By the way, have you been feeding Corduroy?"

"Yeah." Missy tilted her head to one side, her eyes narrowed. It wasn't really an accusing look, yet Shelley felt guilty just the same.

"Thanks. I've been so busy earning money for camp that I forgot."

"That's okay." Missy smiled a thin smile, careful not to stretch her lips. "I like to feed Corduroy. I have all morning anyway." Missy didn't go to kindergarten until the afternoon session.

Shelley stood and stretched. "Last night's paper said three garage sales start tonight. I guess I'll go before everything's picked over." After ruffling both Corduroy's fur and Missy's hair, Shelley went inside to clip the addresses of the sales.

It was a disappointing bargain hunt. All Shelley bought was a miniature World's Fair spoon and a purple plastic belt. At home she added them to her cardboard box, then hunted in the kitchen for something to eat.

"Shelley?" Her mom appeared with a wet Cassie wrapped in a terry cloth towel. "Anna phoned while you were out. You were to call her as soon as you got back."

Shelley brightened. After the frustrating sales,

she'd love some time off for fun. She jogged in place, breathing deeply, while she waited for Anna to pick up the phone.

Instead, Mrs. James answered. "Anna? No, she's gone. Is this Shelley?"

"Yes, I just got home."

"I'm terribly sorry. Anna hoped you could go to the movie at the Orpheum with her tonight."

Shelley glanced over her shoulder, surprised to see it was after seven. "What time does the movie start?"

"It started at six-forty-five. When you didn't call back, Anna and Kendra went ahead and left at six-thirty."

"Oh." Shelley's shoulders slumped. "Please tell Anna I'm sorry." She slowly replaced the receiver.

Her growling stomach reminded Shelley of the time. Judging from the crusted-on plates in the sink, her family had eaten before she got back. At the stove Shelley filled her plate with tuna casserole kept warm on the back burner.

She ran upstairs for her library book, then propped *Blue Willow* against a bowl of apples on the table. She might as well read, since there was no one to talk to. Methodically she spooned in tuna and noodles.

Although Shelley sympathized with the book's main character, she couldn't keep her mind on the story. Eating alone made her feel left out. But, she reminded herself, it was just for a little while longer.

Shrugging, she drained her milk glass and turned the page.

5   Celebrity

ON MONDAY after school Shelley's grinning mother waited on the front step. "Somebody die and leave you a million dollars?" Shelley asked, setting her books on the porch.

"Something better." She squeezed Shelley's shoulders. "We're so proud of you, but you don't have to do this if you don't want to."

"Do what?"

Her mom grinned even wider. "A Mr. McBride called this afternoon. He's a reporter on the *Sentinel*."

Shelley didn't know the name. She rarely read anything but the garage sale ads. "What'd he want?"

"He wants to interview you!"

"*Me?* What for?"

"Isn't there a McBride boy in your class? The reporter said his son was in your grade." She clasped her long paint-stained fingers together.

"Tom McBride's in my class."

"Evidently Tom showed his father the article about you from the school paper. Mr. McBride said you'd make an interesting subject for the local paper." She imitated the reporter's deep voice. "You are a fine example of a young American *entrepreneur*."

"A what?"

"A young business person."

"When does he want to do the interview?" Shelley tried to sound matter-of-fact, as if granting interviews was a normal daily occurrence.

"He'd like to come over tonight and talk with you. He'd also like to take a picture." Her mother leaned against the porch railing. "If that's not okay, I'm to call him back."

Shelley's stomach did backward somersaults. How could she answer a real reporter's questions? Even if it was just Tom McBride's dad, she knew her mind would go blank.

"Will you and Dad stay in the room with me?"

"If you like. I bet you'll like Mr. McBride, though. He sounded like a nice man." She squeezed Shelley's shoulders again. "I love having a celebrity in the family."

"Oh, Mom," Shelley muttered. "I'd better get my homework done now. Do I have to dress up for this picture?"

Her mother studied the threadbare jeans and sweat shirt. "How about a clean outfit? Not dressy, just something decent."

"Okay." Shelley got up, then paused with her hand on the door handle. "If my mind goes blank, will you help talk to this guy?"

Her mother nodded. "Don't worry. You'll do fine."

Shelley hoped so. The article in the school paper had been a nice but unexpected surprise. A genuine interview with an authentic reporter was something else.

Mr. McBride arrived promptly at seven. Dressed in a baggy blue sweater and wrinkled slacks, he talked with her as if he were some polite guest who'd come to visit. From time to time, he jotted notes in a pocket-sized notebook.

Shelley slowly relaxed as the reporter gave her plenty of time to answer his questions. He wanted to know why she'd decided to go into business, where the idea had come from, and what direction she hoped her business would take.

Shelley was stumped at his last question. Where did she want to go from there? Nowhere. After raising forty-five dollars for camp, she intended to go quietly out of business.

And yet, after listening to Mr. McBride's questions, she realized there was no good reason to quit. Not unless she wanted to. Her family was forever short of cash, and a little extra would always come in handy.

It wasn't just the money, either, Shelley admitted to herself. She enjoyed the attention: being asked to find decorations for the band party, Jon's compliment in the school paper, and now an article in the *Sentinel*.

Her thoughts snapped back to the present when Mr. McBride removed his camera from its black case. With faint clicking noises, he adjusted several shiny silver knobs.

"Now, Shelley, I'd like to try both an indoor and outdoor shot of you." First Mr. McBride positioned her in front of their drafty brick fireplace.

Shelley cleared her throat. "Could my family be in the picture too?"

The reporter scratched the back of his neck. "Sure. That's a fine idea."

Shelley shifted to make room for her parents and sisters. Later, her family was grouped outdoors along the porch railing between pots of red geraniums. After the final click of the shutter, Mr. McBride thanked them and left.

Before bed, Shelley called Anna to tell her about the interview, swearing Anna to secrecy. For one thing, she didn't want to sound braggy like trend-setting Charlene.

Anyway, what if the *Sentinel* editor hated her homely photo or thought Mr. McBride's story was too boring to print? At school she half-wished Tom would mention her interview with his dad, but he never did.

Every afternoon Shelley rushed home to search the newspaper. On Thursday she spotted her family's picture on Page Four's "Community News." "Free Enterprise is Alive and Well in Madison" headlined the two-column article. A slowly forming smile lit her face as she read the article word for word.

Her mother tiptoed into the room with Cassie asleep on her shoulder. "Isn't that a lovely article?" she whispered.

Shelley grinned and pointed to the picture. "Look. You can see a little drool on Cassie's mouth."

Her mom chuckled quietly. "Can't win them all. After your father reads the paper, you can cut out the article."

As it turned out, Shelley didn't need to. The next morning when she arrived at school, a copy of the *Sentinel* article was on her desk. The attached note was in Miss Walters's handwriting: "Thought you might like an extra copy."

Shelley slid the article into her desk to reread later. If she were caught staring at her own picture, people would start calling her Charlene.

"Hey, Flash!" Nathan Atkins yelled across the room. "Didn't see you running this morning. Now that you're famous, are you afraid to go out in public?"

Sandra leaned across the aisle. "What's he talking about?"

Before Shelley could answer, Miss Walters clapped her hands for attention. Shelley turned and stared in surprise. Two large Band-Aids crisscrossed her teacher's nose and forehead.

"Get ready for reading," Miss Walters instructed in a nasal tone. The Band-Aid across her nose sounded too tight. "While you do, I'd like to say how proud we are of your success, Shelley. What a lovely article in last night's paper. Tom, your father's a fine writer."

"Thank you, Miss Walters." Shelley stuck her head in her desk and pretended to hunt for her reading book.

Charlene's whiny voice rose over the rustling of papers. "How come *she* got her picture in the paper? We *all* do neat things." She snorted. "What's so great about selling junk, anyway?"

Shelley gasped at the attack. The silence in the room seemed to last forever.

Miss Walters's voice twanged. "Yes, you all do interesting things. As Mr. McBride knows, readers enjoy hearing about enterprising young people who overcome obstacles."

Tom McBride puffed out his chest. "My dad calls them human interest stories."

Exasperated, Shelley felt like the Invisible Man. They discussed her as if she weren't even in the room. When Miss Walters called the first reading group up front, Shelley finally lifted her eyes.

Jon Kruger, wavy hair over his left eye, stared at her from across the room. He bestowed on Shelley a slow, lazy smile, then turned back to his book. Shelley's heart drummed a thundering tattoo under her shirt. Fumbling in her reading book, she tried to concentrate on "The Ox and the Stone."

The rest of the day passed in a blur. That night after supper Shelley shut herself in her bedroom to finish *Blue Willow*. It was one of the best books she'd ever read—she didn't know why it was taking so long to finish. With *Sensible Kate* and *Sarah's Idea* yet to read and her project report to write, she had to wipe out her first book that night.

But as Shelley leaned on her elbows, she couldn't concentrate. After checking the hallway to make sure it was empty, she slid her desk drawer open and pulled out the *Sentinel* article.

She studied the clipping critically. She didn't understand her feelings about it. At school that day she'd felt let down when only Anna, Kendra, and Miss Walters congratulated her on the article. Yet, when the teacher *had* discussed it in class, she'd been embarrassed and wanted them to change the subject.

Shelley returned the picture to the drawer and pulled her box of merchandise from under the bed. Her new box was three times bigger, covered with pink flowered contact paper. An "entrepreneur" couldn't operate out of a battered shoebox.

Sorting through her box, Shelley noted that she was low on her best-selling cheaper items. Time to stock up at the six sales the next morning.

After jogging Saturday morning, Shelley's legs hurt. It had been ages since she'd run a full thirty minutes. Three times last week, she'd had to cut it short. She'd scratched it completely two other days.

Out of breath, she plodded up the driveway. Sweat dripped down the sides of her face as she collapsed on the back step.

Corduroy yapped insistently at the gate. Shelley dragged herself to the backyard to feed and water her dog. At least it was Saturday. Although she wanted to make it to the garage sales, she still had ten minutes.

She tossed Corduroy's favorite chewed-up stick around the yard, then waited while he fetched it for her. "What a life," Shelley mumbled. She fed him two Liver'N'Bacon Biscuits from the sack in the garage. "What a life."

Ten minutes later, Shelley sneaked in the back door. Everyone except Cassie was already up and eating. The clinking of spoons in cereal bowls nearly drowned out the radio.

Missy talked around her mouthful of banana. "Hurry up, Shell. After we eat, I get to help Dad put the life jackets in the car."

"Don't talk with your mouth full," Mr. Gordon said automatically.

Missy waved a half-eaten banana through the air. "Mom fixed chocolate cupcakes with sprinkles on them. Everybody gets two, but if Dad doesn't want his, I get them. I already asked."

Her dad gulped the last of his coffee. "Enough, Missy. Eat so we can get packed up." He tucked in his faded college T-shirt on the way out the kitchen door.

Shelley flopped into his vacated chair. "Where're you going?"

Her mother chopped up onion for the potato salad.

"I told you Dad didn't have to work today. We're taking our swimsuits and a picnic lunch over to Bald Eagle Park."

Shelley scratched her leg. "I don't remember you telling me that." With both hands she pushed her frizzy hair back from her face. "I can't go, Mom."

"What?" Her mom swung around, her wooden spoon dripping mayonnaise. "Of course you're coming."

"I have garage sales to go to this morning. I'm almost out of things to sell or trade, and there won't be other garage sales until next weekend."

"But you love to canoe and swim. I don't want to leave you behind while we all go have fun."

"I don't like the idea either." She loved canoeing with her dad. Their paddles barely made a ripple as they skimmed over the smooth water. If they were quiet, they sometimes spotted beavers or muskrats.

Sighing, she pushed two pieces of bread down in the toaster. "Can I stay home?" Shelley asked. She wasn't sure now if she wanted her mom to say yes or no.

"We'll miss you, but I guess this once would be all right." She reached for a small bowl in the cupboard. "I'll leave some potato salad and fried chicken in the refrigerator and a couple cupcakes—"

A high-pitched scream echoed from down the hall. Shelley jumped up and followed her mother to the living room. In the middle of the floor, Missy wailed like a dog howling at the moon.

"Sweetheart! What's wrong?" Her mother bent over Missy's wailing.

Missy held up her new tennis shoe. "Look what Cassie did!"

Shelley spotted the baby under the coffee table, her eyes opened wide at the commotion. Cassie had learned to roll over and over to get across a room. Evidently she'd rolled under the table and discovered Missy's new shoes.

The shoe laces were soggy from being teethed on. Mrs. Gordon probed Cassie's mouth for the tiny plastic casings she'd chewed off the ends.

Shelley patted Missy's shoulder. "The laces are just a little frayed on the ends. After they dry out, they'll look better."

"But they were brand new!" Missy cried. "See my name printed on the laces? I never even wore them yet." She shook her fist at the bewildered baby. "Now Cassie's wrecked them. She's worse than a dog!"

While her mother packed the picnic basket, Shelley ironed the saliva out of Missy's blue and white shoelaces. Under Missy's suspicious eye, she trimmed off the frayed ends, then pressed the laces flat.

They looked as good as new. Almost, anyway.

Through the kitchen window Shelley watched her father tie the scratched green canoe to the roof of their station wagon. No cheery tune reached her, but she could see he was whistling. Sighing, she gave

Missy her repaired sneakers. If only her *own* problems could be solved as fast as Missy's.

The morning whizzed by. Shelley had become a buyer with a sharp eye, or a "discerning consumer," as Anna's mom said. She seldom spent longer than fifteen minutes at a sale. Only at the largest ones—held by several families so the prices were low and the selection high—did she take longer.

It wasn't hard to guess anymore where she'd be wasting her time. If a young child sat at the cash box, or unmarked clothes of all sizes were jumbled together, or the children's toys were mixed in with the ladies' handbags—Shelley seldom found many bargains.

However, it was great to walk into a sale like her last one of the morning. Held by six families on Cleveland Avenue, it had been worth her time to bike the ten blocks.

The stick-on clothing tags were clearly marked with size and price. Some clothing was neatly folded, some hung on hangers, and all of it was clean. The other items were separated on tables—toys, dishes, records and books. Shelley had easily purchased six low-cost items for her box. She was grateful the saleslady had correct change. Lots of places didn't.

Her box of merchandise teetered on the handlebars as she left. Getting to and from sales—on foot or by bike—often took longer than the actual shopping. Home at noon, she pulled cold chicken and potato salad out of the refrigerator.

Chewing on a gristly piece of chicken, she guessed Missy and her dad were probably paddling the canoe at that very minute. Missy loved water fights and was no doubt flinging cold water at her dad from the end of her paddle.

Shelley shook her frizzy curls and tried to think of something else. She rinsed off her plate, then decided to invite Anna over. They could bake fudge brownies with frosting an inch thick and turn the stereo up as loud as they wanted.

After preheating the oven, she dialed Anna's number. The phone rang four times while she reached into the cupboard for the sugar, cocoa, and shortening. "Anna? Shelley. What are you doing this afternoon?"

Anna sniffed. "You mean *after* I clean my room? And *after* I dust the furniture? And *after* I practice the piano for an hour?"

Shelley took four eggs from the refrigerator. "What are you doing after all that?"

"Probably drop dead." Anna sounded doomed.

"How long will it take to do your chores?"

"About three hours—maybe two if Mom lets me skip that lemon spray polish stuff."

"My parents and Missy and Cassie went to Bald Eagle Park. I thought we could do something while they were gone, but they'll be back by the time you get done." Shelley wound the phone cord around her wrist. "Could we do something tomorrow?"

"I hope so." Anna paused, then screamed into

Shelley's ear. "I'm *coming*, Mom! I have to go. Talk
to you tomorrow."

"Sure. Bye." The line was already dead when
Shelley hung up.

She put back the brownie ingredients, turned off
the oven, and peeled the wrapper from her second
cupcake. One by one, she picked off the colored
sprinkles and popped them into her mouth.

Oh, well, she'd try her other friends, she decided.
But when she called, Charlene was gone shopping
and not expected back for hours. Kendra was baby-
sitting the Nelson kids. Her mother warned Shelley
that Kendra wasn't allowed visitors when she baby-
sat.

Shelley decided she might as well get some work
done. By five o'clock, she'd cleaned everything she'd
bought that morning, using dish soap, silver polish,
and furniture wax. Her shoulders aching, she pushed
her box back under the bed. From under her pillow
she pulled out her new bankbook. It was empty,
except for one entry on the first page.

"At least you're making progress," she said aloud.
"Not terrific, but not bad at all."

The Tuesday before she'd taken twenty-five dollars and opened a savings account at the Fidelity
Bank after school. Six dollars had been saved back
to reinvest in inventory.

The official-looking numbers were impressive.
Shelley couldn't wait to receive her first bank state-

ment. With over three weeks left before the registration deadline, she had over half the money she needed.

On the lonely days, it helped to keep that in mind.

6  Super Salesman

I N TEN SHORT days Shelley's book project was due and she was determined to get going. Sunday night she managed to finish *Blue Willow* by reading under her covers with a flashlight until two A.M. Bleary-eyed, she faced Monday morning. With one book read, she was more confident about the project.

Shifting her cardboard box of merchandise with books stacked on top, Shelley fought against the wind on the way to school. When she finally arrived, she wiped her watering eyes, then opened up shop under an elm tree.

Customers stopped often now, especially collectors like David, Charlene, and Kendra. Other kids stopped too, curious about her "portable garage sale" after the articles in the papers. Evidently advertising *did* pay.

When Anna arrived, Shelley shifted her box to make room for her. "Did you get your chores done Saturday?" she asked, laughing.

"Finally. Then on Sunday we had to visit my Great-Aunt Bertha. What a bore!" Anna dropped her notebook on the grass, then sat on it. "How was yours? Find millions of bargains at the garage sales?"

"I *did* find one really neat thing." Shelley showed Anna a blown-glass golden swan with two baby swans. "I also found a tiny blue bowl you might want to make into a candle."

"That reminds me." Anna dug to the bottom of her shoulder bag. "I have something for you too." She pulled out a small yellow card.

"What's that?"

Anna tossed her long hair over her shoulder. "Mom and I went to the Salvation Army Thrift Store Friday night. A boy at the store gave me this card. I think you should meet him."

Shelley grabbed the card. "Is he cute?"

"*That's* not why you should meet him."

"I knew it was too good to be true." Shelley leaned against the tree trunk. "How'd you meet this guy?"

"While I was looking for cups and saucers, I overheard a boy talking to the cash register lady. He was buying a pile of stuff, but he haggled over the prices—you know, offering her less than the price that was marked."

Shelley nodded. It irritated her when her own customers did that. "Did he get the lower prices?"

Anna nodded. "He also brought a fan and traded it for an old radio and a tiny lamp."

"How'd you see all this?" Shelley zipped her thin jacket. A gust of wind blew sand in her eyes.

"I got in line behind him. After he paid, he handed the saleslady one of these cards." Anna tapped the yellow card with a bright red fingernail. "On the back of the card he listed some things he wanted. He asked the lady to call him if something on his list showed up in her store."

Shelley studied the card. "'Jerome Potter: Barter, Buy or Trade,'" she read. Underneath were a phone number and an address on the other side of Madison. "What did this guy look like?"

"A little older than us. Dressed in slacks and a nice shirt. Wore glasses. Short hair that was perfectly combed."

"How'd you get this card?"

"I just asked him for one. His swapping business and yours sounded a lot alike. I thought maybe you'd like to meet him."

Shelley tapped the business card against her knee. "I doubt if this Jerome person would want to meet me, though. He sounds really successful, and I'm just a beginner."

"Yes, he would." Anna pulled her collar up. "I kind of told him about you. He remembered your picture from the *Sentinel*. He's been selling for three years now and would give you some advice on making more money. You should call him."

Shelley was skeptical. "Did he really say that? About giving me some advice, I mean."

"Yes, if you promise to stay in your own territory."

"If he's been in business for three years, though, I'd be scared stiff to call him. I just started swapping a few weeks ago."

"It's up to you." Anna stood and brushed the dust off her notebook. "I won't mind if you don't call him."

Shelley followed her into the school, thinking about Jerome Potter. He *did* sound successful. He must be, to need a business card.

Cradling her box in her arms, Shelley zigzagged awkwardly through the crowd. Five minutes later, she pushed her box under her desk and took the yellow business card from her pocket. She laid it on her desk and reread it. Imagine being successful enough to need business cards!

She let herself daydream. What if she could do what this Jerome had done? What if her dinky cardboard box business grew into something big? So big *she'd* need a business card someday. The idea made her heart race.

She traced Jerome's name with a polka-dotted fingernail. With a shiver of excitement, Shelley decided she *would* call Jerome Potter. After supper. That very night.

That evening while her mom gave Cassie and Missy baths, Shelley and her dad cleared dirty dishes from the table. She hesitated for a minute, then showed him Jerome's card.

"Do you really think he wouldn't mind if I called him?" she asked, after repeating Anna's words.

"I don't see why not." Mr. Gordon squirted a stream of white dish soap under the running water while he studied the business card she held out. "Jerome Potter. His name does ring a bell."

"But why's he willing to help me? That would increase his competition." Shelley wiped the sticky counters clean.

"Not if you live on opposite sides of town. Plus, if he's older, he probably does business with junior high kids." Her dad studied her thoughtfully. "Say, how's your book project coming along?"

Startled, Shelley avoided his eyes. "I have one of the books read. The other two are pretty short. I can write the paper fast."

Her dad plunged dirty dishes under the suds. "Your mom and I admire how hard you work at your new business. But your schoolwork is more important right now."

"It doesn't interfere. Really." Mentally, Shelley vowed to read at least three chapters of *Sensible Kate* that night.

"Then go ahead and call that young man. It's fun

to talk shop to someone in the same business." He attacked the stuck-on roaster. "But if you decide to meet him in person, it has to be here at our house, when either Mom or I'm at home."

"I doubt if that will ever happen. He can give me advice over the phone." They finished the dishes in friendly silence.

When Shelley hung up her dish towel, her dad said, "I'll work in the garden for a while. Give you some privacy." He winked and nodded toward the phone.

Shelley grinned. "Thanks, Dad."

Armed with paper for taking notes, Shelley perched on the corner of the desk. Taking a deep breath, she dialed. But after only one ring, she dropped the receiver back into place.

She wiped her sweating palms on her jeans. What should she say? How could she begin?

Biting her lip, she picked up the phone again and flexed her fingers. Back and forth across the tiny kitchen she paced, stretching the extra-long cord behind her. Finally, Shelley turned back to the desk. *It's now or never.* Breathing raggedly, she dialed again.

After the fourth ring, a high-pitched voice answered. "Potter residence."

"Um, could I please speak to Jerome?" Shelley asked the girl.

"This is Jerome."

Shelley blinked rapidly. "Oh, I thought— What I mean is, I'm Shelley Gordon. You gave my friend a business card at the Salvation Army Thrift Store."

"Right. Your family had its picture in last week's *Sentinel*?" His voice grew excited.

"Yes. My friend said you, well, would give me some pointers about making more money." She gnawed on her red pencil with the Snoopy eraser.

"Sure. What did you want to know?" His squawky voice became brisk.

Shelley stared at the clean scratch pad. Her mind was as blank as her paper. "I, um, well, do you buy much at the Thrift Shop?" she blurted out. She didn't really care, but she had to say something.

"No, not much. The prices are higher than at garage sales. However, when the store is overstocked, the prices can be negotiated." His voice cracked. He paused, apparently waiting for her next question.

Shelley roamed around the kitchen, tying the telephone cord into knots. *Now what?* She knew she couldn't talk to boys. What had possessed her to call him?

Poking her pencil through her curly hair, she decided to bail out. "Look, I'm just wasting your time. Thanks for offering to help though. It's been nice talking—"

"Wait a minute," Jerome interrupted. "You're not wasting my time." He sneezed twice, then asked, "How about if I ask *you* some questions?"

Shelley chewed her Snoopy eraser. "Okay."

"I assume your business is still a one-man show?"

"One-girl anyway. Why? Isn't yours?"

"Not anymore. Last year I hired another student to help me hunt for garage sale bargains—one who's quite artistic and does my advertising too."

Shelley gulped. "Advertising?" Jerome Potter's Barter, Buy or Trade Shop was a bigger operation than she'd imagined.

"You must let your customer hear about your products. I use various modes to increase public awareness—posters for large sales, printed flyers for a smaller gathering, ads in the school paper." He sneezed again into the phone. "Sorry. When I started out three years ago, I got my picture in the *Sentinel* too. Great free publicity, but that doesn't last after your newness wears off."

He dropped the phone with a clunk. Honks and snorts came over the line as he blew his nose. Then he was back. "Excuse the interruption."

"That's okay." Shelley relaxed. It was hard to be afraid of someone after you heard him blow his nose.

Jerome cleared his throat. "If you're serious about increasing your profit margin, you have to think expansion."

"Expansion?"

"For example, a weekly swap meet at your home can be a good investment of time. Also try swapping at the Legion or Lion's Park where kids hang out on weekends."

Shelley scribbled as fast as she could. She couldn't imagine herself doing any of those things, but she wanted to talk over the ideas with her dad and Anna. "What else?" she said.

"Practice techniques of good salesmanship. For example, if someone says he doesn't want your merchandise, what do you do?"

Shelley scratched her scalp with the pencil. "Um, I say I'm sorry, and maybe next time I'll have something he wants."

"Wrong. When someone doesn't want your product, you have to *make* him want it. Create a demand for your product."

"I didn't know that." *And I couldn't do it in a million years*, she added to herself.

Jerome again sneezed violently. "Excuse me. Now, there are tricks to make your merchandise look its best. The more attractive it appears, the more you can charge for it."

"I always wash and polish my merchandise," Shelley said, relieved that she did do one thing right.

"Good, but that's only the beginning. You must display each piece to its best advantage. Background, lighting, even the arrangement of your items makes a difference."

"Oh." Shelley's head was spinning from all of Jerome's advice. He knew so much and sounded so confident.

More sneezes and snorts were followed by more honks. "Sorry. Let's see. Where were we? Oh, yes, the merchandise isn't the only thing that has to look good. People take you seriously as a business person if you wear attractive clothes instead of jeans and a sweat shirt, especially when selling to adults. You must dress for success."

"To be honest, I'm not sure dressing well would make any difference. I'd like my business to grow, but I'm just not a natural salesman." She sketched pictures of Corduroy on her paper.

Jerome said nothing for thirty seconds. The silence was punctuated by four short, sharp sneezes. "I'll tell you what. If selling is your problem, I could work with you."

Shelley turned as the back screen door creaked open. Mr. Gordon grinned, got a drink of water at the sink, hitched up his loose jeans, then left again.

She recalled her dad's earlier suggestion to invite Jerome to their house. "I would appreciate the help. I don't suppose you could come over sometime this week?"

"How about Thursday? I have your address from the *Sentinel* article."

"Thursday's okay. I get home at four o'clock."

"Four it is."

"By the way, is this all legal? I don't need a permit or anything, do I?"

"It's totally legal. My dad's on the city council, and he says there's no city ordinance banning this kind of business. That is, as long as we're not in permanent dwellings, like the stores downtown."

"Oh. Just wondered. See you Thursday. And thanks."

Shelley replaced the receiver, then raced upstairs with her notes. Flopped down on her bed, she stared up at the ceiling. Jerome's business sounded exciting and successful, no doubt about it. He must spend a lot of time at it. But did she honestly want to get that involved herself?

The rapid fluttering in her stomach told her "yes." A small voice whispered in the back of her mind: "This is your chance to really be somebody."

When Missy somersaulted into their bedroom at nine o'clock, Shelley was snapped out of her day-dreams. She dragged herself to the bathroom to shower and brush her teeth. Although she'd barely moved a muscle for an hour, she was exhausted from her mind racing full speed ahead.

Later, in the dark bedroom, she listened to Missy's soft snores. Her mind whirling, Shelley worked on a tiny piece of mint-flavored dental floss stuck between her molars. She gradually began to relax.

She yawned and curled into a ball, thinking of advertising and dressing for success. Then she abruptly remembered the three chapters of *Sensible Kate* she'd intended to read that night. Groaning, she rolled over and burrowed under the pillow.

"There's always tomorrow," she told herself as she drifted off to sleep.

1 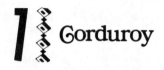 Corduroy

SHELLEY SLEPT fitfully that night, her dreams filled with sneezing super salesmen. Awake by five A.M., she pondered Jerome Potter's advice. When the sun finally rose, she was too tired to make herself jog.

In class that morning, Shelley daydreamed as she stared out the window. She couldn't wait to meet Jerome on Thursday, but she was a little scared too.

"—and how are *you* coming along, Shelley?"

Shelley jerked around in her seat, knocking her stapler to the floor. At the front of the room, Miss Walters waited politely. Emily Sayers and Suzie Beck watched her and giggled.

Shelley smiled at her teacher and gulped. "Excuse me?"

Miss Walters pointed to a chart on the blackboard. "We were discussing the book projects. I asked how yours was coming along."

"Oh. I'm still reading, but I'm almost ready to write the paper." Shelley kept smiling, hoping she looked as if she were telling the truth. Emily Sayers giggled again.

Well, she argued with herself, she *was* still reading the books. And she *did* hope to start her paper soon. She had to. In a week the project was due.

Miss Walters's words whistled slightly. "That's fine. I imagine most of us are still reading. This sample chart on the board should help you organize your report."

Miss Walters jabbed the blackboard with her rubber-tipped stick. "Down this side of the chart you list the books you've read."

Jab, jab, jab, went the pointer down the side of the chart.

"Across the top you write these words: characters, themes, and conflicts."

Jab, jab, jab.

Miss Walters shouldered her pointer like a rifle. "If you fill in the blocks on the chart, it will be simple to compare the three parts of the different books."

Shelley's mood brightened as she studied the chart. She'd draw one right after school. Then, while reading *Sensible Kate* and *Sarah's Idea*, she'd fill in the chart as she went. When the books were finished, the chart would be complete. To write her paper, she'd simply copy from her chart.

Relieved, she leaned over and grabbed her stapler. Her dad was right. She worried too much.

That night Shelley found a large piece of cardboard to use for her chart. Using heavy markers, she divided the chart into nine large squares. She neatly lettered the book titles down one side and the categories across the top.

"There." She tilted her head to one side. "Very professional looking, if I do say so myself."

As she tossed the markers into her desk drawer, she spotted the school paper article and the photo from the *Sentinel*. She pulled out the articles, now smudged, and curled up on the bed to reread them.

A heady sense of importance welled up inside her. She'd carefully avoided any mention of the articles in front of her friends, so they wouldn't think she was conceited. Privately, though, she loved to reread them.

"You know something else? He gobbles oatmeal cookies up but spits out chocolate chip ones!"

Shelley's feet hit the floor with a thud. Missy's excited chatter drifted down the hallway. Hearing her mom's voice, Shelley shoved the articles under the bed.

Missy bounced into the room, pulling on her mother's hand. "You wait and see. His tricks are going to be the hit of the show."

"No doubt. But are you sure Corduroy should eat grapes and cookies?" Mrs. Gordon tickled Missy's bare foot.

"Food works lots better for rewards," Missy said firmly. She tucked her bare feet under her pillow. "A rubber bone didn't work at all."

Her mother turned on the Donald Duck night light. "What works the best?"

"Orange popsicles! Corduroy sits up and begs real good when I wave one under his nose."

Shelley pitched her pillow across the room at Missy. "So *that's* where my popsicle went!"

The week before, Shelley'd agreed to let Missy enter Corduroy in her kindergarten pet contest. Considering how often Missy fed the dog these days, it was a small favor.

Mrs. Gordon tossed Shelley's pillow back. "Say, aren't you about ready for bed?"

"I didn't know it was after nine already." She laid her chart on the bed. With her new reading lamp attached to her headboard, it would be easy to work in bed while Missy slept. "'Night, Mom."

Mumbling to herself as she brushed her teeth, she planned her weekend. "If I work like crazy, I'll get both books read and the chart filled in by Monday. That'll leave me three whole days to write my paper." She rinsed her mouth one last time.

A few minutes later she crawled into bed. Working steadily for an hour, she filled in the character, theme, and plot categories for *Blue Willow*. At ten-thirty, she placed her chart carefully on the floor and snapped out her reading light.

Lying in the darkness, Shelley tried to think of

questions to ask Jerome on Thursday, but she kept drifting off. Finally she gave in. She could think about her list while she jogged in the morning.

But she overslept again and had to gobble her raisin toast on the way to school. She'd had no time to fix her wildly curly hair, and she tried to flatten it with her hands as she reached the school building.

That night Shelley worked in her room, stopping only ten minutes for supper. First she listed a page of questions to ask Jerome. Then she polished her merchandise to look its best. Shelley suspected Jerome Potter's inventory sparkled.

She wondered how Jerome would look when he arrived at her house the next afternoon. Wouldn't it be romantic, Shelley daydreamed, if he were tall and handsome? Then, someday when they were both famous entrepreneurs, they'd be photographed together. Then, of course, their pictures would appear on the *front* page of the *Sentinel*.

The next afternoon, Shelley dashed out of the school building before the final bell had stopped ringing. Her breath came in gasps by the time she arrived home, fifteen minutes before Jerome was due.

First she set up her merchandise in the living room, trying different arrangements to make it look impressive. In the kitchen she fixed a quart of lemonade and sliced half a loaf of banana bread in case Jerome was hungry.

At the last minute she changed into a clean T-shirt,

one her aunt had mailed while on vacation. Glittery orange letters on her back promised "It's Better in the Bahamas." Maybe Jerome would think she'd been on a world cruise.

Shelley glanced at the clock. Two minutes till four. After rearranging some jewelry again, she stationed herself behind the living room curtains.

Jerome was still halfway down the block when Shelley spotted him. Anna'd been right. From his light blue shirt and creased navy slacks to his shiny black shoes, he was the image of a successful businessman.

Shelley opened the front door before he could ring the bell. "Hi. Are you Jerome?" She braced the door open with her jogging shoe. "I'm Shelley Gordon."

"Hi." He carefully wiped his polished oxfords on the rug. "Nice to meet you." Jerome strode across the room to the table where Shelley had her merchandise arranged. "Is this your total inventory?"

"I'm a little low on, um, inventory, right now. I plan to pick up several things this weekend."

He nodded vigorously. "Using your capital to build adequate inventory is costly at first. However, it's a business expense, just like advertising." He whipped a spotless white handkerchief from his shirt pocket and dusted the tiny crevices in Shelley's cut-glass candy dish.

"I don't have much, um, capital, to, uh, reinvest in inventory." The business terms sounded strange to Shelley's ears. "What I really need is tips on selling. Something you said on the phone made me curious."

"What was that?" Through his black-rimmed glasses, Jerome's eyes appeared glazed. A faint sheen of perspiration glistened on his upper lip.

"You said if a customer didn't want a certain item, you had to *make* him want it." Shelley shook her head. "But how?"

Jerome waved his handkerchief in the direction of the end table. "Tricks of the trade. Whatever you want to sell, the techniques are basically the same." He refolded his handkerchief along its creases and tucked it into his pocket.

"Like what?"

"For one thing, act interested in your customers. Ask them questions. People love to talk about themselves."

"How does that sell anything?"

"It lays the groundwork, so to speak. Always call your customers by name. With some people, just a casual touch on the arm has them eating right out of your hand." Jerome nodded vehemently. "That's just the beginning."

Shelley was intrigued. "Then what?"

"Flattery works miracles, especially with adults. Call an old lady young, or pretend you think her daughter is her younger sister. That nearly always works." He ticked off the points on his clean stubby fingers. "With young girls, it works the opposite.

A junior high girl is flattered if you seem to believe she's in high school."

Shelley frowned. She didn't think she'd feel comfortable doing that. "I still don't get—"

Jerome strutted around the room, his voice growing more intense. "Then, when you have them in the palm of your hand, you can sell them anything." He pivoted on his heel. "Here, I'll show you."

He scrutinized her merchandise. Tapping a finger against his chin, he finally selected a cameo Shelley'd found in the tornado room. She'd never been able to sell it.

While Jerome studied the cameo, Shelley's mom peeked around the corner of the living room. Shelley smiled uncertainly and was relieved when her mom returned to the kitchen.

Jerome came toward her, muttering to himself. Shelley shifted around, suddenly not wanting him to read that it was "better in the Bahamas." She figured Jerome wouldn't find it very business like.

"Now, let's pretend I want to sell you this blue and white cameo." He cleared his throat noisily and dropped his voice an octave. "Good morning, Shelley. Did you just get back from vacation? I'll bet it was beautiful in the Bahamas."

Shelley winced. "Yes, it was . . . lovely." Her face grew warm. If any of her family overheard them, she'd die.

Jerome stepped closer. "I have something here you'll love. When I bought this cameo from an elderly lady last week, I thought of you immediately. Cameos will always be in style."

Shelley took the necklace he held out. "That's very pretty, but I hardly ever wear jewelry."

"Oh, but you should! The robin's egg blue of the cameo is the exact shade of your eyes." He held the brooch near her cheek. "You should definitely wear blue. It makes your eyes enormous."

Embarrassed, Shelley's face burned hotter. "Well, yes, well, thank you," she stammered. "I guess I will buy the cameo."

Triumphantly, Jerome rocked high on his toes. "*Voila!* If this were a real sale, I'd move in now and clinch the deal before you could reconsider."

Shelley marveled at Jerome's self-confidence. "Those techniques may work for you, but . . . " She shook her head as her voiced trailed off.

"Sure you could! It only takes practice." Jerome wiped the film of perspiration from his upper lip, then snatched a feather duster from the table of merchandise. "Here. Sell this to me."

"I can't." Shelley gripped her hands behind her. "What could I say? That these ostrich feathers are the exact shade of your eyes and you should dust more often?"

Jerome smiled, but continued to hold out the feather duster. "You must practice if you want to learn the art of salesmanship."

Reluctantly Shelley took the feather duster. Strok-

ing the gray feathers, she closed her eyes and concentrated. There must be *some* fantastic selling points
about feather dusters. Finally, though, she gave up
and tossed the duster on the couch.

"You make it look so easy, but I don't know what
to say."

"Selling is easy for me because I've been at it
three years. You just need more training. This is
what you should do." Jerome whipped out a pad and
pencil from his pocket, wrote on the pad, then ripped
off the top sheet and handed it to Shelley.

"What's this?" Shelley studied the neat handwriting.

"The date of the Y's annual giant flea market
coming up. It's a real goldmine for swappers like
you and me." His shining eyes gleamed as if he'd
slipped into a trance. "This is my third year to have
a booth. I think you should come."

"How would this flea market help me?"

"You could sit in my booth and watch me in action.
You'd learn more that way in an hour than by days
of role-playing." He dabbed at his moist face with
his handkerchief. "What do you say?"

Shelley studied her mounds of unsold merchandise.
If she could learn to sell as well as Jerome, she'd be
able to unload it all. And that would put her on the
road to Forest Lake.

Shelley took the plunge. "Thanks, Jerome. I'll be
there."

Jerome broke into a grin and shook her hand. He'd never be handsome, Shelley thought, but when he smiled he wasn't half bad.

That evening, with her head still whirling from her afternoon with Jerome, Shelley curled up in the bean-bag chair with her second book by Doris Gates. She concentrated through three chapters, dutifully making notes on her chart.

By bedtime she'd made good progress in *Sensible Kate*. She crawled gratefully under her quilt. Moments later, just before falling asleep, she remembered the lemonade and banana bread in the kitchen.

Coming home from school the next afternoon, Shelley collided head-on with Missy as she hurtled out the back door. "Hold it!" Shelley caught Missy by the shoulders. "What's going on?"

"Corduroy won! Corduroy won!" Missy hopped in circles, waving a blue ribbon with FIRST PRIZE lettered on it.

"What'd he win a ribbon for?"

Missy's red football helmet slipped over her eyes as she stamped her foot. "Our pet contest was today."

"Sorry. I forgot." Shelley inspected the handmade ribbon. "That's pretty. What tricks did Corduroy do?"

"Come here. I'll show you!" Missy bounced on her tiptoes around to the backyard. "Sit over there."

Shelley folded her long legs beneath her and sat

on the grass. Arching her back, she enjoyed the sun's warmth on her face. Relaxing for a minute felt great.

Friday afternoons *used* to be her favorite time of the week. With school over until Monday, leisurely weekends had stretched out before her. But lately, Friday afternoons meant the beginning of a working weekend: hunting bargains at garage sales and cleaning merchandise.

Shelley leaned forward eagerly as Corduroy came bounding across the yard. How good it would feel to play with Corduroy again, rolling around and wrestling on the grass. Until Shelley watched the beautiful dog racing toward her, she hadn't realized how much she missed him.

But it wasn't to Shelley that Corduroy ran.

Instead he sprang into Missy's outstretched arms, knocking her over onto the soft grass. Giggles and barks mingled as they tumbled on the grass.

Shelley watched wistfully. Corduroy seemed to consider Missy his owner these days.

Missy scrambled to her feet. After a deep bow, she demonstrated what she'd taught Corduroy for the pet show. He rolled over, played dead, and sat up. Shelley applauded loudly, then got up to leave.

"No, wait a minute! I saved the best trick till last."

Missy began to sing "Where, Oh Where, Has My Little Dog Gone?" in a high pitched screechy voice. Corduroy crawled behind her on his stomach. Then he lay flat on the ground, covering his ears with his paws.

Shelley whistled and cheered. "That's really funny! I can see why you won first prize."

Missy curtsied daintily, her football helmet slipping sideways. "Thank you, thank you. No applause. Just throw money."

Grinning, Shelley picked up her school books and went inside. She wished she could sit longer, soaking up the sun, but she had a million things to do. For starters, she'd better study the ads to see which sales started that night.

After supper she pedaled off down the street. At a large yard sale, she hunted quickly through card tables stacked high. A child's bright red ball caught her eye. Thinking of Corduroy, she picked it up. A bell inside the ball tinkled.

Since it cost only thirty cents, Shelley dropped the ball into her shopping basket. Corduroy should love this new toy. Then, Shelley hoped, maybe he'd remember who his *real* owner was.

At home later, she found Corduroy behind the garage. Coaxing him, she held the ball high and made the bell tinkle. He jumped and yipped excitedly until she tossed him the ball. Shelley managed to stroke his fur once before he loped away. Shelley laughed and chased him until he disappeared inside his doghouse.

Bending over, she peered in and was surprised to find Missy.

"Hi, Shell." Missy crawled out on hands and knees. "That's a neat ball you got Corduroy."

Missy heaved the ball Corduroy dropped at her feet. The dog tore after it, bringing it back to her. Missy tossed it again. Corduroy nosed it out from under a tomato plant and again carried it to her.

Although Shelley repeatedly called to her dog, he didn't seem to hear. Giving up, she finally trudged inside. Neither Missy nor Corduroy appeared to notice.

Taking a huge wedge of leftover chocolate layer cake upstairs to her bedroom, Shelley assured herself that soon she would be less busy. In another couple weeks, she'd have time to sit and play with Corduroy too. Then things would return to the way they had been.

Swallowing a large mouthful of cake, Shelley nodded her head firmly. It was only a matter of time.

8 Dress for Success

LYING IN BED Saturday morning, Shelley gave herself a pep talk. She needed to get up and get started on the seven garage sales listed in the newspaper. After a brief struggle, she rolled out of bed and landed on the floor with a thud.

To relieve her stiff leg muscles, Shelley decided to take ten minutes for some calisthentics. But after fifteen toe-touches and twenty sit-ups, she was winded. A month ago, she knew, that much exercise would have been a snap. Giving up, she headed for a shower.

As she combed her wet hair, Shelley sprayed water droplets across the mirror. She loved how much longer her hair looked when it was wet. However, in half an hour, Shelley knew her dried hair would frizz

wildly around her face. She would have given anything for straight hair to wear in French braids like
Anna's.

Sliding the *Sentinel* picture from her desk drawer,
she studied her black and white image. What was it
Jerome had said? *"To be taken seriously as a business
person, you had to dress for success."*

Jerome had viewed her photograph with horror,
she suspected. With the "I Love My Dog" T-shirt
and frizzy hair that framed her face, Shelley knew no
one would expect her to turn up on Wall Street.

Shrugging, Shelley cut the sale ads from the paper
and left. On her way out the door she grabbed a sack
that contained two blueberry doughnuts. Not too
nourishing, maybe, but there was no time for more.

Two and a half hours later she returned. Her bike
wobbled on its flat tire.

What a crummy morning! She'd hunted through
junk at five garage sales before running over a
smashed pop bottle. Only one of the sales had been
worth her time. The others were dinky and un-
organized and strung across town. She'd spent most
of her time getting from one sale to the next.

After the flat tire, she'd given up and started home.
Walking her bike to the last two sales was impossible.
One sale was over a mile away.

Back home, she washed her greasy hands after
changing the flat tire. With a glance in the mirror,
she stopped short at her bedraggled appearance. From

her plastered down, curly hair to the hole she'd ripped in her shirt, she looked anything but a picture of success. She was glad Jerome couldn't see her now.

She turned away from her frumpy image and went downstairs for lunch.

In the kitchen Missy poured milk into root beer mugs while her mom made sandwiches. In her infant seat on the kitchen counter, Cassie slobbered on a celery stick.

"What's for lunch?" Shelley asked, wiggling Cassie's bare toes.

"I fixed meat loaf sandwiches out of the leftovers." Her mother slathered the meat with ketchup, then added the top slice of whole wheat bread.

"Mom?" Shelley asked. "Do you like having curly hair?"

Her mother cut the sandwiches in half. "I do now, although at your age I hated it. Why?"

"I'm sick of looking like a witch all the time." She lifted Cassie to her shoulder, careful to support her back.

"I remember feeling that way too." Her mom studied her. "You really do have lovely hair. Some day you'll appreciate the curls."

"I doubt that. Nothing I've tried will tame them."

Her mom laughed suddenly. "When I was in college, I had my hair straightened one year. The girls in the dorm ironed each other's hair."

"*Ironed*? Didn't that hurt?"

"Not as long as the iron didn't touch your scalp."
She set the sandwiches on the table. "However,"
she added, shaking her head, "I finally grew to enjoy
having natural body and bounce. You will too
someday."

"Maybe." During lunch, Shelley said no more
about it, but her mom had given her an idea. Why
couldn't she straighten her own hair? The effects of
ironing wouldn't last long, but maybe she could get
a commercial straightener sometime at Bergman's.

That afternoon while everyone napped, Shelley
sneaked the iron up to her room. She wanted to iron
a small piece of hair to see if she liked it before
spending hard-earned money for a straightener. If
the result was horrid, she'd just get her hair wet.
The curls would reappear in no time.

Preheating the iron on "wool," Shelley spread
towels over her desk. When the iron was hot, she
pulled her dampened hair straight and bent over.
Her hair lay across the towels.

With a wary eye fixed on the iron, Shelley brought
it close to her head. Cringing, she lowered it to her
stretched out hair. She snatched her fingers back and
slammed the iron down.

Ssssss hissed the iron when hot metal touched wet
hair.

Shelley hardly breathed. After a few seconds, she
lifted the iron and raised her head. The hunk of
ironed hair was no longer curly, merely wrinkled.

To Shelley's eye, it wasn't much of an improvement.

"Guess I need to hold the iron down longer," she muttered.

She redampened her hair and tried again. Lowering the iron, she counted carefully. "One thousand one, one thousand two, one thousand three, one thousand four, one thousand five."

At the end of five seconds, Shelley lifted the heavy iron and grinned at her reflection.

This time the hair on her right side was almost perfectly straight. It contrasted sharply with the curly left side. Straight hair definitely gave her a more serious look. Riotous curls belonged around the faces of clowns.

Half an hour later, she finished. Her right arm ached from holding the heavy iron. But where reddish curls had bounced, now straight russet hair hung nearly to her shoulders. She twirled in front of the mirror, admiring the way it flew out from her head.

"This is just the beginning," she announced. "Now—to dress for success."

Until Jerome had explained how important her image was, Shelley'd loved reading the *Sentinel* article. Now the photo made her cringe. However, at the flea market in two weeks, she'd show Jerome her new image.

In her closet, Shelley rummaged through her tangled hangers for a successful-looking outfit. Jeans and shirts were out—too informal. On the other hand, her church dresses looked too serious.

"What about those gray pants Aunt Karen sent me for my birthday? Where are they?" she mumbled. They'd be perfect, worn with her white sweater with the lacy collar.

She finally found them, crushed in the back of the closet. Kicking off her shoes, she slipped on the wrinkled gray slacks. She sucked in her stomach, but the nylon zipper jerked to a stop halfway up.

Irritated, Shelley lay flat on her back on the bed, then tugged again on the zipper. That did the trick— the pants zipped easily.

When she stood up she could barely breathe. Posing before the full-length mirror on the back of her bedroom door, she groaned at her reflection.

The wrinkled pants cut in at her waistline, leaving soft lumps above and below the narrow gray belt. Bulges at her thighs stretched the fabric tight, erasing the wrinkles there. Shelley felt sick. Just two months ago she'd tried on those pants, and they'd fit fine then. She couldn't have gained that much weight!

Peeling off the slacks, though, she recalled how often lately she'd skipped her morning run. Most days she'd had barely enough time to grab a bite to eat on the way to school.

What she'd grabbed wasn't too great either, she knew. Doughnuts, cookies, bread—whatever was handy.

As she hung up her slacks, she vowed she'd jog again every morning and eat more balanced meals.

In two weeks those slacks *had* to fit. Nothing else she owned was suitable for the flea market.

Shelley completely overhauled her meager wardrobe the next day. To dress for success, she'd have to skip her T-shirts and cut-offs, except to wear at home. Her jogging shoes would be saved for running, but she'd wear sandals the rest of the time.

All Sunday afternoon she mixed and matched her best-looking clothes. From two pair of pants and three blouses, she created five different coordinated outfits for school.

She also treated herself to a pair of tortoise shell barrettes she'd bought on Saturday. She'd intended to sell them to Charlene, but Shelley decided she needed them worse herself.

As she tried the barrettes at various angles, Shelley thought about her parents' reaction the day before. When she'd come down to supper in her newly straightened hair, her dad's eyebrows had jumped alarmingly. But after she turned a complete circle for him, he said he liked it.

Her mom pronounced it "becoming," but asked to do the ironing herself in the future. She didn't want Shelley to scorch herself.

Remembering her vow, Shelley went to bed promptly at eight-thirty that night. Early Monday morning she dragged herself out of bed to jog. She met Nathan Atkins at her usual spot. "Hey, Flash, what'd you do to your hair?" he yelled across the street.

Shelley bit her lip. She'd have to get used to that question. Another thing—her nickname had pleased her before, but now it didn't sound at all businesslike. *Flash Gordon* was not a name you connected with high finance.

Shelley walked slowly to school that morning in her stiff sandals. The straps cut into her ankles. In blue slacks and a plaid blouse, she *did* feel more businesslike. After jogging, she'd had to touch up her hair with the iron, and she enjoyed the feel of her straighened hair as it brushed her shoulders.

Shelley paused at the edge of the crowded school yard, practically the last person to arrive. Ladylike walking was a pain—it took forever. With a shaky breath, she joined the girls gathered under her favorite tree.

"Hey, Flash! Who stole your curls?" David Forest shouted. "Say, did you find any pocket knives this weekend?"

"No, the sales were lousy. I'll try again next weekend." Shelley shifted her box of merchandise to her other hip.

Anna whistled softly. "What *did* you do to your hair? It looks super!"

Shelley beamed. "Do you really like it? I ironed out the curls!"

"Ironed it?" Kendra's laugh came out like a snort, making her choke. Her eyes watered as she doubled over. "You're kidding!"

Shelley's face grew warm. "My mom said she

ironed her hair in college, so I tried it. It's fun for a change." It shook her confidence, seeing the girls' mouths hanging open.

Charlene smoothed her own perfect haircut. "Well, it's certainly a change, all right."

Slightly deflated, Shelley was grateful when the buzzer rescued her from further questions. She trailed Anna into the building.

"Good morning, Shelley!" Miss Walters said, beaming. "It seems we both visited the hairdresser this weekend."

Shelley stared at her teacher's transformation. Miss Walters's formerly chopped-off straight hair now curled gently around her face. Her teacher looked amazingly younger. Maybe appearances were even more important than Shelley had realized if someone like Miss Walters was making such an effort, too.

"It might've been simpler if we'd just traded hair," Shelley said, fingering the tortoise shell barrettes.

Miss Walters chuckled. "How true! Your hair looks lovely. I always liked your curls, but I do understand how a change can be fun." She patted her curls. "A person can get bored looking the same all the time."

"That's for sure." Shelley smiled, then limped to her desk. She collapsed gratefully and massaged her sore ankles.

As the morning passed Shelley's confidence grew. Two more girls admired her new hair style. Even Jon stopped on his way to the pencil sharpener, whispering, "I like the change." An hour later, Shelley still glowed.

Jon's words replayed in her mind all day. Her confidence mounted, until just ten minutes before the dismissal bell. Then all thoughts of clothes and success and Jon were erased from her mind.

Miss Walters clapped her hands for attention. "Just a reminder, class. The day after tomorrow is the due date for your book project."

Cold sweat broke out on Shelley's forehead.

Peggy Jenkin's hand shot into the air. "If we're not done, can we hand in the chart and finish the paper later?"

"I don't think so." Miss Walters shook her fluffy hair. "Since you've had over three weeks for the assignment, I won't accept any late papers. If you don't hand in a paper on Wednesday, I'll have to give you an incomplete for your English grade."

Shelley tried to swallow the lump in her throat. Where had the time gone? Over the weekend she'd intended to do so much reading. But every minute had been taken: she'd worked on her hair and wardrobe, exercised, bargain-hunted at garage sales, and patched her bike tire.

Immediately after school she raced home, ignoring the pain in her raw ankles. She'd finish *Sensible Kate* that night if she had to stay up till dawn. She shouted, "I'm home, Mom!" as she burst into the kitchen.

She expected to find her mother where she did most afternoons, refinishing the old oak table. The chipped green paint was finally gone, and she was in the process of sanding the curved table legs smooth. But today the sandpaper scraps lay scattered under the table.

"Shelley?" Her mom's voice drifted down the stairs. "Come up to Cassie's room. I need a favor."

Shelley took the stairs two at a time to her baby sister's tiny room. Using rainbow-patterned wallpaper, her mom had converted the walk-in closet to a nursery. She now sat in the rocking chair, Cassie cradled in one arm.

"What's up, Mom?"

"I just took Cassie to the doctor." She stroked the baby's forehead. "Her temperature hit 103 this afternoon. You know how fussy she was all weekend."

Shelley nodded. She'd heard her parents up with Cassie four or five times the night before. "What did you want me to do?"

"Dr. McGivern called in a prescription for an antibiotic. Cassie has an ear infection." She spoke louder over Cassie's sudden wails. "Could you bike down to Bergman's and pick it up for me?"

"Sure." She had a million things to do, but she couldn't say so. "I'll change clothes first."

She scrambled into jeans and T-shirt, jumped on her three-speed, and raced to the drug store. The prescription wasn't ready. Tapping her foot impatiently, she waited while the druggist typed the bottle label. Back home, she handed her mom the slim white pharmacy sack with the medicine in it. "Here's your change too."

"Thanks, honey. I hope this helps soon. Unless I hold Cassie constantly, she screams at the top of her lungs."

"Her ears must hurt a lot." Shelley was anxious to get to work in her room. "If that's all you need—"

"Actually, I could use your help with supper. If you could start it, Dad can finish when he gets home from work." Her mom rubbed a weary hand across her forehead.

"Well—"

"Make a salad and brown the hamburger for spaghetti sauce," she called over her shoulder, then disappeared into Cassie's room.

"But, Mom . . . " Shelley's voice trailed off. Oh, what was the point? Anyway, her mom couldn't help it that Cassie was sick.

She hurried to the kitchen and shouted through the screen door. "Missy! Hey, Missy!" No answer. She stepped outside and yelled louded. "Melissa Sue Gordon, come here!"

After several seconds Missy poked her head out of Corduroy's doghouse. "What do you want?"

"Come set the table for supper. I have to cook."

"In a minute." She disappeared back into the dog house.

Shelley hurried back inside. While the meat browned, she shredded lettuce into a large bowl. So far, there was no sign of her dad. She added the tomato paste and herbs for the sauce. Ten minutes later Missy finally came in to set the table. Still no dad. Shelley buttered the drained spaghetti. Supper was ready by the time her dad pulled in the driveway.

"Sorry I'm late, everybody." He kissed Shelley and Missy. "Where's your mom?"

"With Cassie. She has an ear infection." Her father headed for the stairs. "Tell Mom supper's ready," Shelley called after him.

That night Shelley bolted her meal without tasting it. When she carried her plate to the sink, her dad said, "Go ahead and do your homework, Shelley. Supper tasted great."

"Thanks. I *do* have to work on my book project."

Upstairs, Shelley spread her three library books and chart across the floor. The chart's section for *Blue Willow* was filled in, but that was all. She'd read three chapters of *Sensible Kate*, but could only fill out a bit of the character section.

"Wish I'd taken speed reading," Shelley muttered.

She opened to Chapter Four of *Sensible Kate*. Reading steadily for an hour, she jotted down five lines in the plot section. At the end of Chapter Seven she glanced up, amazed to see Missy already in her pajamas.

"What time is it?"

"Eight o'clock." With a flying leap, Missy crash landed in the center of her bed. "Mom said you have to take your shower now."

Shelley flipped through the rest of the book and groaned. Even if she read until she was cross-eyed, she'd never be able to finish *Sensible Kate*, let alone *Sarah's Idea*. And the very next night she had to write her project paper.

Shelley's stomach churned. What could she do? She'd always worked hard on her schoolwork, but this time she'd have to cheat. Just a little.

Opening the book, Shelley studied the blurb on the inside of the dust jacket. Four short paragraphs gave a fair idea of the book's plot. Using the short summary, she hastily filled in the squares for *Sensible Kate*.

Next she read the jacket of *Sarah's Idea*. She was surprised the jacket blurbs were so complete. If she faked it here and there and relied heavily on the book she'd actually read, Shelley thought she could write a decent project paper.

At twenty minutes past eleven, she crawled wearily into bed. Her chart lay on her desk, all the squares filled in. Her overdue library books were stacked by the door to return the next day.

She'd write her paper immediately after school on Tuesday. No sweat.

Trying to unwind and fall asleep, Shelley couldn't quite shake the guilt that lay in the pit of her stomach. She'd never cheated on schoolwork before.

"I won't do it again," she whispered to herself in the dark.

Plumping up her pillow, Shelley vowed not to get

behind schedule again. She'd read *Sensible Kate* and *Sarah's Idea* the very first chance she got. That way it wouldn't *really* be cheating.

As soon as I earn my camp money, she promised herself, *life will calm down*. Sighing, she rolled over and tried to believe it.

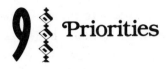# 9 ❖ Priorities

ALL NIGHT LONG, Miss Walters's face loomed in Shelley's troubled dreams. No matter where she hid, her teacher's stare convinced her she knew all about the faked report. The next morning Shelley staggered out of bed, exhausted from thrashing around all night.

To shake the gloomy feeling and get back in shape, Shelley tied her jogging shoes and tiptoed down the creaky stairs.

Her usual half hour of jogging took forty-five minutes. A stitch in her side forced Shelley to stop three times. She leaned against a maple tree, breathing raggedly. Shelley was both disgusted and embarrassed.

Back at home again, she checked on Cassie, who was sleeping peacefully. Shelley was glad the antibiotic had worked fast. Then, still determined to lose her extra weight, Shelley fixed a plain bagel and poached egg for breakfast.

After dressing hurriedly, Shelley grabbed her box of merchandise. "Shop and Save with Shelley" was lettered on the side. Arms full, she squeezed out the kitchen door and started down the driveway.

"Shelley Gordon, come back here!"

Missy's shrill voice pierced the early morning stillness. She hung over the backyard fence, still in her pajamas. In one hand was a bag of dog food; in the other, Corduroy's dish.

"What do you want, Missy? I'm already late." Shelley kept walking backwards down the driveway.

Missy followed, her bare feet slap-slapping the pavement. "You wait a minute! I want to talk to you about *your* dog."

Puzzled at her anger, Shelley asked, "What about Corduroy?"

Missy waved the dog dish under Shelley's nose. "Do you know how long it's been since you fed Corduroy, or gave him some water?"

"No, not exactly."

"A zillion days! Weeks!" Missy's eyes narrowed to slits.

Shelley blinked rapidly. She knew it *had* been a long time, and now, thinking back, she realized it had been more than two weeks. How could she have forgotten for over two weeks?

"I'm sorry, but you know how busy I've been."

"It's not fair that I do your chores every day for free." Missy flattened an ant with her bare foot. "Corduroy's *your* dog."

"I know he is," Shelley snapped, glancing at her watch. She was fifteen minutes late already. "What do you want exactly?"

"Since you make so much money now, you should pay me to baby-sit Corduroy. One dollar a week. I'll feed him and water him and walk him every morning."

"A whole dollar?" Shelley calculated quickly. "Well, okay, but it won't last long. I almost have enough money for camp. Then I'll take care of Corduroy myself."

Missy turned on her heel and dragged the bag of Bow Wow Chow up the driveway. "I want this week's dollar tonight after school," she called over her shoulder.

"Okay, okay. I've got to go now." Shelley hiked down the sidewalk, her thoughts already turning to her book project.

That night Shelley raced home after school, changed out of her school clothes, and pulled on her pajamas. Until bedtime, she intended to use every spare minute on her project paper.

With her chart propped upright on her desk, she studied it carefully. It wasn't easy to compare the one book she'd read with the two she hadn't. However, the book jacket blurbs had helped a lot.

If she used lots of examples from the book she'd actually read, Shelley found she could just hint at events from the unread books. But would it fool Miss Walters? Shelley was staking her English grade on it.

By eleven-thirty that night, Shelley's mom insisted she turn off her lamp. Shelley didn't argue. Her eyes were nearly crossed after three hours of writing.

She stacked her papers, careful not to rustle them too loudly. Missy, after collecting her dollar, had been asleep for three hours already. Shelley slipped her four neatly written pages into a yellow folder, rubbed her eyes, and collapsed into bed.

After school the next day it was a relief to finally forget about her book project. There was business to conduct.

Mrs. Roberts, who lived at the end of High Street, had asked Shelley to hunt for small statues for her yard. On Saturday Shelley'd found two things her neighbor "just adored": a green frog sitting under an orange toadstool; and a red hen with three yellow chicks peeking out from under her wings.

Personally, Shelley wouldn't be caught dead with those dumb statues in her front yard. However, Mrs. Roberts was willing to pay four dollars each. As they'd only cost Shelley a dollar apiece, she'd make a fast six dollars upon delivery.

After school Shelley lugged the frog and hen outside to scrub. Armed with a bucket of sudsy water and a wooden scrub brush, she worked at the picnic table.

Beyond the garden Missy and Corduroy played fetch with a rubber T-bone. Hearing all their shrieking and yapping, Shelley envied them. She had scoured the first yellow chick when her mom yelled out the kitchen window. "Shelley! Telephone!"

Shelley dunked the hen in the bucket of soapy water to soak, then ran into the kitchen. "Hello?"

"Shelley? It's Anna. I had a great idea!"

"What's that?" Shelley twirled around, winding the long cord around her knees.

"Let's celebrate finishing our book projects. Mom said she'd take us roller skating right after supper tonight."

"Right after supper?" Shelley paused, her shoulders slumped. "I can't. Remember the frog and chicken I found for Mrs. Roberts last Saturday? I deliver them tonight."

"That won't take more than ten minutes. It's only six now—we'll pick you up at six-thirty."

"I still have to clean those dirty statues." Shelley twisted the phone cord around her finger and watched it turn purple. "I won't be done for at least another hour." Anna sighed heavily into the phone. "You going skating anyway?"

After a short pause, Anna asked, "Would you mind if I asked Kendra?"

"Go ahead." Shelley chewed her bottom lip. "Have a good time."

"Okay, if you're sure. See you in the morning."

After a faint click, the dial tone returned. Shelley

trudged back outside where she scrubbed and scoured for the next forty-five minutes. At supper time the frog and chicken family perched on the picnic table, clean and rinsed. Shelley left them in the setting sun to dry while she ate.

After supper, she used Missy's red wagon to deliver the statues. "Shelley, they're perfect! Aren't they?" Mrs. Roberts demanded.

"Yes, perfect." Shelley tried to sound enthusiastic.

"I *am* the first on the block to have statues, you know. In no time, you'll see them up and down High Street. They're all the rage." As Mrs. Roberts nodded vigorously, her red bandana head scarf flashed up and down.

"I'm sure they will be." Shelley hesitated. She always hated to ask for payment. "Well, I should go . . . "

"Wait. Here's what I owe you."

"Thanks!" Relieved, Shelley put the eight dollars in her pocket. It made her feel better about missing out on the roller skating.

At home in her room, Shelley added the eight dollars to the bank on her desk. The number in her bankbook would grow even bigger when she deposited the cash. Shelley was glad she was getting closer to her goal. Having no free time was driving her nuts.

She hated feeling so left out. Corduroy now preferred Missy. Her best friend was skating with Kendra. All she ever did was work, work, work. She hoped *somebody* noticed how bravely she gave up all her fun.

Slowly a new thought forced itself into her mind. What if nobody noticed what a huge sacrifice she was making? She'd been too busy lately to even feed her own dog or see her best friend. Suppose Anna and Corduroy felt she was *ignoring* them? She could see how it might look that way.

She frowned and hugged her pillow to her stomach. *Just what I need. One more thing to feel guilty about.*

She didn't want her friends and family to think she was ignoring them, but there wasn't time to do the things she wanted. Still, maybe there was a way to make it up to them.

As she pedaled around Madison Saturday morning, Shelley searched for different things to buy with the five dollars in her pocket. This splurge would dent her camp fund a little, but she couldn't help it.

By ten-thirty her gifts were carefully packed in her bike basket: a glittery red dog dish for Corduroy; an old blue porcelain cup and saucer for Anna's candle-making; a sturdy garden trowel for her dad; a jump rope for Missy; and a set of fruit-shaped refrigerator magnets for her mom.

Shelley nodded with satisfaction. That should cure any hurt feelings. Back home, she presented her gifts to her family with a flourish.

"Thanks, Shell!" Missy swung the red-handled jump rope around the kitchen.

"Outside with that, Melissa," their mom ordered.

"I love these new magnets, honey. I'll use them for all my notes and Missy's art work. But it wasn't necessary."

"I know. I just wanted to." Shelley handed the trowel to her dad. "I thought this would work better than our old chipped hoe."

"Sure will, but I hope you didn't spend too much of your hard-earned money for it. I know the deadline to sign up for camp is getting close." He ruffled her hair, curly again from the high humidity.

"I'll have enough."

"You deserve to have a great time at Forest Lake. You've worked awfully hard." Her dad brandished his trowel like a sword. "Guess I'll go see how this works. I still have some cauliflower plants to set out."

In previous years Shelley and her dad had planted the entire garden together. This year, though, all she'd had time for was the marigold border. She hadn't even checked to see if the flowers had come up yet.

"Wait. I'll help you plant," Shelley said suddenly.

"Great. I'd love the company." Her dad held the kitchen door open and Shelley ducked under his arm.

In the garden Shelley discovered her marigold seedlings had pushed through the ground. The sharply notched leaves were thick. Unfortunately, so were the weeds. Shelley knelt to yank at the weeds and encroaching crabgrass.

Her dad hummed off-key while he dug holes for the cauliflower plants. Shelley watched him from the corner of her eye. How could he sound so happy? His life was so boring.

"Dad?" Shelley sat back on her heels. "Doesn't anything ever bug you?"

"Bug me?" He wiped his face with a wrinkled handkerchief. "Sure. I get irritated at times, like everyone else."

"Does it bother you to work all the time? You go to work, you come home and help Mom, you grow the garden, you mow grass, you wash the car." She searched for just the right words. "You don't ever have any fun."

He pulled on one ear lobe thoughtfully. "I really don't mind my job. And I enjoy working around the house, at least most of the time." He dug another cauliflower hole. "You're not really talking about me, are you?"

"What do you mean?"

"Aren't you talking about your own life? You have school, homework, swapping, your chores in the house." He poured half a bucket of water into the hole. "Don't *you* have fun anymore?"

Shelley avoided his eyes as she crawled beside the marigold border. "Life *has* been the pits lately."

"For instance?"

"Well, Anna used to wait for me to do stuff. She doesn't anymore. When I can't go somewhere right away, she invites Kendra." Shelley tossed a handful of weeds over her shoulder. "It's not *my* fault I've been so busy lately."

"True." He moved across the garden, filling each hole with water. "Maybe it doesn't need to happen so often, though."

Corduroy bounded across the yard and jumped on Shelley's back. "What do you mean?" she asked, ruffling the dog's fur.

"Remember last week when you missed our picnic?" At Shelley's nod, he said, "I could have stayed home too and set out the cauliflower plants then. They wouldn't be so wilted today if I had."

"Then why didn't you? Mom would have understood."

"It seemed more important to spend time with my family." He waved his arm across the backyard. "As you can see, the grass needs mowing today too. I had to choose between the cauliflower and the yard. What's most important right now? Planting the garden. I can always mow grass—it isn't going anywhere."

Shelley nodded. She just wished her decisions were as simple as choosing between cauliflower and grass.

Shelley helped her dad fill in the soil around the roots of the small plants. "I have to make money for camp. I don't have the choices you talked about."

"You've already made your choice—to put earning money above everything else." Her dad wiped his muddy hands on the grass. "I just hope you don't get hurt."

"How could I get hurt?"

"By having no time for your schoolwork and your

friends." He grasped Corduroy firmly by his collar and dragged him from where he was burying his rubber T-bone. "You can't do everything without eventually wearing yourself out. Someday you'll have to choose what's most important to you. Try making a list—friends, family, school, selling—then rank them in order of importance."

"How?" Shelley asked. They were *all* important to her.

"There's no one right way. Everyone chooses differently. You have to decide what's important to *you*."

"Then what?"

"Then comes the hard part. Put first things first. If you decide Anna is more important than your selling, for example, you'll make more time for her." He stood and stretched after placing the last tile.

Shelley crawled back to her marigolds. "I suppose so." She proceeded down the row, her mind on her dad's words.

Her friends and family *were* important to her. She already knew that, without making any list. Shelley ripped up a handful of crabgrass. Luckily she wouldn't be so busy much longer. Then her priorities would just naturally fall back into place.

That would be a relief. Things sure seemed out of balance now.

10  Backfire

LOST IN THOUGHT, Shelley missed the weeds and yanked out three marigold plants.

Her dad's words made sense. Yet they were the exact opposite from Jerome's advice about success in business. Wasn't there some way to find time for everything important to her?

Abruptly Shelley sat back on the grass. Of course! Why hadn't she thought of it before?

Jerome told her to expand her business, but that meant working even more hours than she did now. A few minutes ago, her dad had said she should make more time for Anna, if their friendship was important. Why not do both things at once?

Shelley brushed the dirt from her hands. "I have to do something, Dad. I'll finish this border later."

"Sure, run along. I'll be here quite a while yet."

"Thanks." Shelley ran toward the house. In less than five minutes, she was washed up, had grabbed her paper bag, and was on her way to Anna's.

Anna opened the door at Shelley's impatient knocking. "Hi. What's going on?"

"I had a terrific idea, and I wanted to talk to you about it right away."

"We can't talk privately inside. Mom and her bridge friends are playing today." Anna slipped outside. "Let's sit on the step."

Shelley plopped down beside Anna. "I'm so busy lately that I don't have much time to do things with you. We hardly ever talk anymore."

"No kidding!" Anna quickly added, "But you're working so we can go to camp together. I understand."

"I *could* make money and see you at the same time." She scratched at the dried mud on her knees. "That is, well, what if you worked for me? Jerome has people working for him—doing advertising, selling, stuff like that."

Anna fingered her long braid. "But you know I can't draw, so advertising is out. And remember when I had to sell five band concert tickets last year? I *did* try, but I ended up buying them all myself. That door-to-door stuff is not for me."

"That's not what I had in mind."

"What then?"

"You know about the things some kids at school have asked me to hunt for. The pocket knives, the beads, the South Seas decorations."

"That stuff is practically sold when you take it to school."

"Right. But I could use some help hunting for the stuff. I'd give you a commission on whatever you find that I sell later."

"I do go to lots of sales already," Anna agreed as her eyes lit up. "And we could work together cleaning the stuff we buy. It *would* be fun."

"Great! I'll give you five dollars to invest. Then we'll take what wc find to school." Shelley pulled a crumpled five-dollar bill from her jeans pocket before Anna changed her mind.

Anna rolled the bill into a cigar-shaped tube. "I could start this afternoon. Even if things are picked over already, I can still practice hunting for the popular stuff."

Shelley lifted the blue porcelain cup and saucer from the paper sack. "Here. I found something for you today."

Anna ran her finger around the rim of the cup. "This will make a beautiful candle!"

"I thought so too." Shelley paused. "Working together's going to be great. You'll see. Look out, junior cabin, here we come!"

Shelley saluted as she jogged backwards down Anna's driveway, then turned and headed up High Street for home.

On the way home, Shelley's mind raced faster than her feet. Why hadn't she thought of this simple solution before? Solving the problem with Anna had been a cinch. Her dad made setting priorities sound so hard, but it wasn't.

Her mom said she always wanted to have her cake and eat it too. Why not? With a little planning, she could have her business, her friends, and good grades besides.

That night at eight-thirty Anna's voice bubbled over the telephone wire. "Shelley? I got some really neat stuff!"

"What'd you find?"

"A miniature pocket knife on a key chain for David. A cute little doggie raincoat that Sandra will love for that spoiled-rotten dog of hers. Plus lots of other neat things to make some instant money."

"Can I come see everything tomorrow afternoon?"

"I already asked." Anna sighed loudly. "Dad said Aunt Marion and Uncle Luke will be here tomorrow. I have to *entertain* my three bratty cousins so the adults can 'hear themselves think.'"

"Yuck." Shelley shifted her grape jawbreaker to her other cheek. "I guess I can wait till Monday. Bring it all to school."

After Shelley replaced the receiver, she grabbed a handful of carameled popcorn from the bowl on the table. Anna'd sounded so excited. Maybe she should reletter her box: Shop and Save with Anna and Shelley.

On Monday, however, Shelley's enthusiasm died when she saw how Anna'd spent the five dollars. The miniature knife was unusual with its carved handle. But when Shelley pulled out the blade, it was rusty and the tip was broken off.

Shelley avoided Anna's eyes. "Um, did you notice the chipped blade when you bought this?"

"Yes, but when it's folded in, it doesn't even show. The handle is the pretty part. I doubt if David ever opens the knives he collects." Anna rewrapped the knife in brown paper. "You can show it to David later."

Shelley clenched her jaw, biting back her answer. David *did* inspect the knives he bought, very closely.

Her thoughts were interrupted when Sandra marched around the corner of the building.

"Sandra!" Shelley called. "You're just the person we wanted!" She lowered her voice. "Now's a good time to show her the doggie coat you found. Where is it?"

"In this sack. Here, you tell her about it."

"Why don't you show it to her? She's wild about that mutt of hers. Should be an easy sale."

Anna chewed the inside of her cheek. "I guess I could try." She took a deep breath as Sandra advanced toward them.

"What's up?" Sandra halted in front of them.

"Uh, well, I thought, that is . . . " Anna stammered. She pulled a red plaid doggie rain coat from her grocery sack. "I knew you'd love this the minute I saw it." She held out the tiny garment for Sandra to inspect.

"What's it supposed to be?"

"A raincoat for Princess!" There was a hint of panic in Anna's voice. "With this, even during the rainy summers, Princess can get enough exercise."

Shelley nodded, pleased. A doggie raincoat was something she'd never have bought. With Anna's help her merchandise would have more variety, she could see that.

Sandra studied the coat inside and out. "This is pretty, and Princess' old one *is* worn out." She handed it back.

Anna pulled on her bottom lip. "But don't you want to buy it? It only costs a dollar."

"Excellent price for a coat," Sandra agreed, "but it fits a small dog, like maybe a poodle. Princess is a golden Lab. That little coat would barely make a rain hat." She pivoted sharply and marched toward the school building.

Anna stuffed the doggie raincoat back into her sack. "I guess I blew it. From the way Sandra talks about her 'sweet little darling,' I thought Princess was a tiny mutt."

Shelley gritted her teeth. Except for Sandra, she didn't know another soul who acted so sappy over her dog. Where would she unload that dumb thing now?

"Don't worry about it," Shelley said. "You'll have better luck with the other things."

However, it got worse instead. As Shelley had feared, David wouldn't pay a good price for the rusty knife. He did finally give Anna fifty cents, but she'd paid a dollar for it.

Anna retreated further into her shell as the day wore on.

No one was persuaded to buy the plaid doggie rain coat, a fake emerald stick pin, or a coin purse with the name "Marie" stamped on the back in gold letters.

Kendra did buy a string of glass beads for a dime more than they had cost. Mr. Krebb, the janitor, also bought a pocket-sized address book. By the time the dismissal bell rang, Anna's sales totaled a loss of forty cents.

Walking home after school, Shelley tried to encourage her. "Don't worry. This was just your first day. Remember when I started? I didn't do so hot either."

Anna's feet dragged down the sidewalk. "But I *lost* you money. Maybe this wasn't such a good idea after all."

"Don't give up yet." Shelley tried to sound enthusiastic. "I have to see Mrs. Roberts tomorrow after school. I'm going to try to sell her some wooden windmills for her flower beds. Come with me."

"Why?"

"Then I can show you what Jerome taught me about selling. You'd only have to watch. You don't have to talk or anything."

"All right." Anna stopped at the corner where their paths divided. "I'm really sorry I lost you five dollars. I'll pay you back."

"You worry too much. We'll sell the things you bought." Shelley tried to convince herself as much as Anna. "See you tomorrow."

The next afternoon Anna followed Shelley home after school. Upstairs, Shelley recombed her straightened hair. Satisfied with her successful image, she picked up a wooden Dutch windmill and handed one to Anna to carry.

"Did Mrs. Roberts ask you to look for these?" Anna twirled the white wooden cross at the top of the windmill.

"No," Shelley admitted, "but I decided to take a chance. Jerome says you can make a customer buy what you have to sell."

"Even if she doesn't want them?" Anna asked.

Shelley didn't miss the doubt in her friend's voice. "I hope so. Anyway, I'll give it a shot."

They lugged the three-foot-high red-and-white windmills down High Street. When they arrived, Mrs. Roberts was fertilizing her lawn, her back to the street.

"Hello, Mrs. Roberts," Shelley called out. "How are you?"

Her neighbor whirled around, her hand on the fertilizer spreader. "Oh, hi there, Shelley. You startled me."

Shelley set her windmill on the sidewalk. "I was just admiring your yard."

Mrs. Roberts surveyed the velvety looking lawn. "It *does* look lovely, doesn't it? The frog and chickens you brought me last week add just the right touch, don't you think so?"

Shelley nodded. "They do add a lot of personality to your yard." Shelley took a deep breath. "I biked down Lexington Avenue the other day. The yards on that street are spectacular."

Mrs. Roberts sniffed. "All those rich people have gardeners. No one can compete with that."

"That's true," Shelley said, following Jerome's advice to agree with the customer first, "but many of their flower gardens looked just like yours."

"They did?"

"Yes." Shelley frowned slightly. "Except for one thing."

"Except for *what* one thing?" Mrs. Roberts demanded.

Shelley avoided Anna's eyes, afraid she would laugh. "The flower gardens in front of those expensive homes had little Dutch windmills in them. A breeze blew that day, and the windmills looked so colorful as they turned."

"Windmills like those on the sidewalk?" Mrs. Roberts asked.

"Just like them. I bought those windmills at a yard sale near Lexington Avenue."

Lips pursed, Mrs. Roberts squatted on the sidewalk and inspected the two windmills. Shelley was glad she'd scrubbed them clean, then touched up the trim with some leftover red paint.

"Are these windmills for sale?" Mrs. Roberts asked casually.

Shelley glanced triumphantly at Anna, who stood on the sidewalk, her mouth hanging open. Shelley swallowed the giggles that bubbled up inside her, then turned to Mrs. Roberts.

"Yes, they sell for five dollars each. For this week only, you can get two for nine dollars." Shelley wandered casually around her neighbor's yard, smelling the lilacs and tulips, admiring the bridal wreath in bloom.

"Two for nine, you say?" Mrs. Roberts stood up. "I'll take them. Wait here, and I'll get the money. These will be perfect in my tulip beds, don't you think?" She nodded sharply. "Very Dutchy."

"You'll be the first on our block to have them," Shelley replied.

Mrs. Roberts nodded grimly. "We'll show those rich people on Lexington Avenue that you don't need a gardener to have beautiful flower beds."

When the front door clicked shut, Anna ran over to Shelley. "I can't believe it," she whispered. "You were terrific!"

"Thanks." Even Shelley was amazed that Jerome's

advice had worked so well. "Let's put these ugly windmills on the front step."

"Shelley, do the houses on Lexington Avenue really have windmills in their front yards?"

Shelley avoided Anna's gaze. "I did see one house with a windmill," she said defensively. "I'm sure there are others."

Anna was silent as they hauled the windmills to the step. Her stillness grated on Shelley's nerves.

"Look, I didn't *lie* to her. Jerome says this is a common selling technique to make your product more desirable." Shelley shifted uncomfortably. Even in her own ears, her excuse sounded weak.

She was interrupted as Mrs. Roberts reappeared with the nine dollars. As the girls walked back to Shelley's house, she calculated quickly. "Hey! I only need *one* more dollar for camp!" she shouted.

Anna's braids flew out as she whirled around. "All right! We can sign up Monday night after school." After a long pause, she added, "After watching you with Mrs. Roberts, I know I could never sell like you do."

"What do you mean?"

"I'm just not that . . . brave."

"But you only started today! I was terrified at first too."

"I think it would *always* scare me to death. Anyway, since you've earned enough money now, you don't need me."

Shelley sighed. "Are you sure?"

"I'm not cut out for this," Anna said quietly, staring at the sidewalk.

"That's okay. Like you said, I finally have the money for Forest Lake. We'll have lots of time together from now on."

"You're not mad?"

"No, I'm not mad. See you tomorrow." Waving the nine one-dollar bills, Shelley turned toward home.

The end of the week passed in a blur for Shelley. She couldn't wait till Monday to sign up for camp. But, she realized, going to the Y's flea market on Saturday sounded almost as exciting.

On Friday afternoon, Shelley's daydreams about her business were interrupted by Nathan's poke in the ribs. Miss Walters stood at the head of the aisle, balancing a large stack of papers on her arm.

"Yuck, our book projects." Nathan jammed his hands in his pockets. "Great way to ruin a weekend."

Shelley's breathing grew ragged. After she'd turned in her project report, she'd pushed her guilty feelings to the back of her mind, but now . . .

What if she hadn't been so clever after all? What if her teacher had guessed she hadn't read two of the books?

Miss Walters cleared her throat. "Before I hand out these project papers, I want to say what a fine overall job you did. These were most interesting and insightful."

When she smiled, Shelley noticed the huge gap between her two front teeth was no longer there. Her whistle when she talked had also disappeared.

"As you know," Miss Walters continued, "this book project is a major portion of this quarter's English grade. Most of you did very well, and I enjoyed reading your ideas."

With a smile, she started down the aisle. Sometimes she stopped to comment on an especially good paper or a favorite book.

As Miss Walters inched closer, Shelley wiped her hands on her cotton slacks. Although she wasn't an *A* student, Shelley'd never been afraid to face her teacher before.

At last Miss Walters reached her desk and handed Shelley her stapled papers. "A lovely job, Shelley. You chose one of my favorite authors."

Shelley arranged her stiff lips into a smile, then glanced at the top sheet of paper. *B+!* She couldn't believe it. Looking up at her teacher, she grinned broadly. "Doris Gates is my favorite author now too."

Miss Walters perched on the edge of Shelley's desk. "I remember crying when Leo was killed in *Sensible Kate*. Wasn't that sad?"

Shelley blinked quickly. She'd read Leo's name on the jacket blurb. Was he Kate's new dad? No— maybe her fishing friend? "Yes, it was awfully sad," Shelley finally said.

Miss Walters tilted her head thoughtfully. "I

admired Kate when she left that birthday party because it was boring. It took courage not to do what
everyone expected of her."

Shelley wished desperately that Miss Walters
would get off her desk and move down the aisle. She
couldn't keep nodding all day, afraid to open her
mouth. What dumb luck to choose books her teacher'd read.

Miss Walters patted her shoulder, then got up
and handed Nathan his paper. Shelley heaved a sigh
of relief. Her teacher started down the aisle, then
turned around.

"What did you think of Nora?"

Shelley's head jerked up. Was Miss Walters talking to her or Nathan? She swiveled in her seat and
met her teacher's direct gaze. Miss Walters waited
expectantly.

Shelley gulped hard. The name "Nora" sounded
familiar, but she couldn't place her. A knot of fear
coiled in Shelley's stomach.

Nora, Nora. Who *was* she?

Her teacher spoke again. "She was a perfect adoptive mother for Kate, don't you think?"

Kate let out the breath she had been holding.
Adoptive mother. Of course.

"Yes, she was just what Kate needed all right."
She remembered from the four chapters she'd read
that Kate was an orphan. "Kate needed a responsible
person to take good care of her."

Shelley watched as Miss Walters's smile slowly

faded. A small vertical wrinkle appeared between her eyebrows. "What makes you think Nora was a responsible person?"

"Well, I thought that to adopt a kid, you had to be able to take care of her," she mumbled.

Miss Walters looked sad. "In real life, I'm sure that's true. But in *Sensible Kate*, Nora's helpless. So Kate felt needed in Nora's house, especially with their new baby coming." Her words trailed off. "If I remember correctly," she added softly.

Shelley looked down at her hands. Her pounding heart almost echoed in the hushed room.

"See me after school please, Shelley," Miss Walters said. She moved down the aisle, passing out more papers.

Shelley stared blindly at the B+ on her project paper. She refused to look around the room, afraid to see Anna's pity or Charlene's snobby sneer. After an eternity, the dismissal bell rang. While her friends noisily filed out the door, she pretended to rearrange her erasers and colored paper clips.

A pair of pink-and-maroon suede shoes stopped beside her desk. "Too bad you got caught. I got an A on my project paper." Charlene stooped to tie her shoelace, giving Shelley a perfect view of her project paper. Sure enough, a big red A blazed across the top. "Good luck with Wart Face," she whispered, then hurried to catch up with Jon.

'Wart face'! How unfair to someone who'd just given her an A. Anyway, those moles were gone.

Miss Walters had been on a "dress for success" campaign of her own.

In a few minutes, the hallways were silent. After the three school buses roared away outside, Miss Walters walked wordlessly toward Shelley. She dragged Nathan's desk close and sat down.

"Did you read the books, Shelley?" she asked.

Shelley gulped. "Not all three of them. Just *Blue Willow*, plus a few chapters of *Sensible Kate*."

"I wish you'd told me you were having problems with the project. Is there a reason you weren't able to finish?" She sounded genuinely concerned.

Shelley sat hunched over, remembering how much time she'd spent bargain hunting, cleaning merchandise, jogging, trying to "dress for success," and helping out at home. Not being able to finish her project was no mystery. There just hadn't been enough hours in the day for everything.

She placed hands flat on the desk top. "I did try, but I just ran out of time," she finally said.

"I'm sorry, Shelley, I really am. You're a fine student, but you know that I can't give you a B+ now."

Shelley slid the stapled papers across to Miss Walters, who crossed out the grade on her paper.

"You'll have to do this over, after you've read the other two books. Being late will cost you some points, I'm afraid. I'll give you another week to finish. If it's not done then, you'll get an incomplete in English for the year."

Incomplete? She glanced at her teacher, but Miss Walters looked almost as sad as Shelley felt herself. An "incomplete" on her report card would mean summer school to make up the English grade. Summer school meant no Forest Lake.

"I'll do the project over." Shelley cleared her throat. "I'm sorry, Miss Walters."

"I am too." Her teacher rose, smoothed down Shelley's frizzy hair, then walked slowly back to her desk.

Shelley gathered up her pile of books for the weekend. She'd intended to head straight home after school to choose her clothes for the flea market the next day. Sighing, she decided she'd better detour to the public library instead.

There were a couple of books she was dying to read.

11 Flea Market

WHY DO I FEEL like such a failure?" Shelley mumbled aloud that night as she lay on her bed.

For a girl who'd been so successful lately—earning her camp money, getting her picture in the paper— she felt as if she'd disappointed everyone she cared about.

As she chewed off her long thumbnail, Shelley recalled Miss Walters's disappointment that afternoon when she'd learned about the cheating. And, of course, there was Anna. Their long, lazy hours together after school had long ago been replaced by business. Working together had seemed like such an ingenious solution to the problem.

"What a bomb that was." Shelley tossed the slivers of fingernail under the bed.

She'd even failed Corduroy. Paying Missy only reduced the guilt a little.

Flopping over on her stomach, Shelley listed the good things about her swapping. "Going to camp is first on my list. Plus getting to buy presents for the family." Silently, she added a third reason—the special attention she'd received at school.

She sat up and hugged her bare knees. "Is it really worth it?" she asked her reflection in the mirror across the room.

She rarely had time to jog anymore, never played with Corduroy, seldom saw Anna or Kendra, and couldn't even get her schoolwork done on time. Maybe her dad had been right after all that day in the garden. Putting first things first *was* hard.

However, there was no doubt about one thing. She had to redo her book project within a week or she'd go to summer school instead of Forest Lake. Shelley knew her dad felt school came first; with an incomplete English grade, her swapping days would be over.

Padding downstairs to the kitchen, Shelley filled a mug with root beer. She grabbed four oatmeal-raisin cookies, then trudged back up to her bedroom. She intended to read at least half of *Sensible Kate* before going to sleep, but she needed incentive.

She shut the bedroom door to drown out the TV, then began. The time passed quickly as she read one chapter after another. She barely glanced up at nine-thirty when her dad tucked Missy into bed. He kissed

Shelley and picked up her empty glass, then left. Since it was Friday, Shelley knew she could read as late as she wanted.

By eleven-thirty, when rubbing her eyes no longer kept the print from blurring, Shelley'd read seven chapters. She snapped off the reading light and smiled tiredly in the dark. She *would* finish the books this time.

The next morning Shelley woke with a knot of excitement in her stomach and cookie crumbs in her bed. She couldn't wait to go to the flea market that afternoon.

Missy skidded into the room and crashed against the bed. "Shelley! Dad's taking us to the water slide park after lunch!" Her football helmet's mouthpiece bobbed up and down where it hung loose. "Mom said Mrs. Sutton'll baby-sit Cassie so all four of us can go on the slides!"

Shelley grinned, but shook her head. "I can't go. That flea market's this afternoon."

"I thought you already had enough money for camp. Don't you?" Missy's accusing tone caught Shelley by surprise.

She sat up and stretched. "Yes, I have enough money, but I promised Jerome I'd come. That reminds me. Since I have time now, you don't have to feed Corduroy anymore."

Missy glared at her. "Even if you feed Corduroy, it's *me* he loves now. I'm the one who plays with him."

Shelley winced. "When you're older, you'll under-stand how busy people can get. You're just a baby now."

"I am not! Anyway, just because you're older doesn't mean you can treat people rotten!"

"I'm not treating anybody rotten!" Shelley snapped, sick of Missy's lecture.

"You are too." Her eyes blazed through the face guard on her football helmet. "Going to the water slide park was Dad's reward for you earning all that camp money. Now we probably won't get to go." She pivoted on her bare heel and stalked off down the hall.

Shelley flopped back on her pillow. Missy sure had a lot of nerve. What did she know anyway? She was just a squirt in kindergarten.

Even so, Shelley had trouble swallowing her sand-wich at lunchtime. It kept sticking in her throat. Her parents hadn't complained about canceling the outing, but she could see the disappointment in her mom's face.

Shelley knew she'd gone to a lot of trouble, getting a sitter for Cassie and all, but she knew she'd told her mom about the flea market a whole week ago. At least she was pretty sure. It was too bad if her mom had forgotten.

When she reached for the chip dip, Shelley was "accidentally" stabbed by Missy's fork. Frowning, Shelley rubbed her fork wound. She knew Missy was mad about not going. Shelley decided to look for something nice for Missy at the flea market that afternoon.

Like a muzzle, maybe.

After lunch she dressed carefully for the flea market. She'd ironed both her hair and clothes that morning, and her new successful image should surprise Jerome.

Half an hour later the city bus deposited Shelley one block from the YMCA-YWCA. Although she was twenty minutes early, the parking lot was already jammed. Bikes and baby strollers were sandwiched in between cars.

Inside, Shelley squeezed through the crowded entrance to the flea market. Pushing around a mob of browsers, she zigzagged past displays of ceramic dolphins and quilted pillows.

"Oops, I'm sorry." Shelley turned to the woman whose toes she'd just smashed. Without a word, the woman shoved Shelley aside and continued through the crowd.

Past three more stalls and around the corner, Shelley finally spotted Jerome's booth. It was squeezed in between two tables—one piled high with second-hand books and one displaying hand-painted pottery. Jerome looked so businesslike in his navy jacket and tie. Her voice squeaked. "Hi, Jerome."

He barely glanced up. "Hi, Shelley. Can you get through there?" He motioned toward the end of the table. "Great crowd, don't you think?"

"I *am* surprised," she admitted. "Have you sold anything yet?"

"No. For the first half hour, customers circulate and compare prices for the best bargains."

"Oh." Shelley stood with her hands behind her back.

Jerome wiped his glistening forehead with his handkerchief. "Don't worry, though, they'll be back." He studied his artfully arranged display. Shelley noticed four large cardboard cartons under the table were still full.

Jerome's banner across the back of the booth challenged buyers to "Shop and Compare—Lowest Prices Anywhere." A green glass dish near the cash box held a stack of his business cards.

Hoping she didn't look nosy, Shelley peeked in the boxes under the table. Three cartons held items similar to those on the table. The fourth box held colored wrapping paper, white tissue, and bows.

Jerome did gift wrapping? That was something she'd never thought about.

Jerome's "salesman" voice drifted down to where she squatted. "This sequined belt is a must for the high school Spring Fling. It's a Fifties dance this year, you know. These belts, worn with circle skirts, were all the rage in the Fifties."

Shelley peered over the table between two tall vases and stifled a laugh. Jerome was trying to sell the belt to a girl Shelley knew from school. It would be ages before that fifth grade girl was invited to a high school dance.

"Jerome," she whispered, "that girl's only—"

He spoke louder, drowning out Shelley's voice. "The emerald green sequins accent the green in your eyes." Jerome held the belt out to the blushing girl. "With a white or green skirt, it would look terrific."

"Oh, I don't know . . . "

Jerome raised one eyebrow. "You *are* going to the Fifties Dance, aren't you?" His tone implied that surely such a gorgeous girl had a dozen dates to choose from.

"I . . . I probably will." The girl hesitated. "Just three dollars?"

"Correct." In one smooth motion, Jerome snapped open a small sack and slipped the girl's money into the cashbox. "Have a wonderful time at the dance."

Slowly Shelley stood up. The plump fifth-grade girl clutched her sack and smiled shyly at Jerome, then moved reluctantly down the crowded aisle. Jerome filled the empty space on the table with an Indian beaded belt.

"Do you know who that girl was?" Shelley asked. "She was just a fifth grader from my school."

"And?"

"She's not going to any high school Fifties dance. She's too young."

Jerome's round face was genuinely puzzled. "So? I knew that."

"But you said—"

"She was flattered that I thought she was in high school." He rearranged a porcelain teapot, creamer, and sugar bowl. "Remember what I told you? Old ladies want to believe they look young. Young girls like to think they look older."

Shelley glanced down the aisle. She couldn't help feeling sorry for the fifth grade girl, even though no one had forced her to buy the belt.

Shelley watched Jerome as he rearranged his glassware. Most of Jerome's sales practices were great, but a few were kind of shady, it seemed to her. Shelley shrugged—she didn't have to do *everything* he did.

Jerome brushed tiny flecks of dust from the table. "If you want to sell, study human nature. Figure out what a person wants, then try to sell it to him."

For the next two hours Shelley watched Jerome in action as people, eager to buy, crowded the booth. He sold a musical Teddy bear to a mother with a screaming baby in her backpack. He assured the frazzled young mother that the musical tones, resembling human heartbeats, were designed especially to soothe cranky babies.

Shelley listened in amazement when he sold an ugly pair of pewter candlesticks to some newlyweds. He pointed out the intricate design in the candlesticks and the durability of pewter. Shelley cringed when he talked about romantic candlelight dinners for two.

Reaching under the table, Jerome brought out a box of long tapered candles. "What's your favorite color?" he asked the young woman.

"Blue, because it's John's favorite color." She

slipped her hand through her young husband's arm.

Jerome unwrapped two new blue candles and positioned them in the holders. "The color sets off the pewter to perfection."

"Oh, John, wouldn't they look elegant in our living room?"

"I'll add the candles at no extra cost," Jerome added smoothly.

The husband shrugged, then reached for his wallet. "If you like them, Sweetheart, we'll get them." He handed Jerome a ten-dollar bill.

Jerome patted his shiny forehead as the couple moved down the aisle. "Ten dollars," he whispered to Shelley. "I only paid three for those dirty old things. They cleaned up rather well, though, don't you think?"

Shelley nodded, amazed how easily he'd made a seven-dollar profit. After another hour of watching Jerome sell one item after another, she unpacked more merchandise from the extra boxes.

Jerome stepped to the back of the booth. "Now it's your turn."

"My turn?" Shelley rearranged necklaces and rings on Jerome's black velvet cloth. "To do what?"

"To sell something. Watching is instructional, but nothing beats experience."

"I can't do what you do," Shelley protested, ashamed at her panicky tone of voice. "I'd just lose you money."

"I'll be right here if you need help. Do you want

134 · FIRST THINGS FIRST

your business to be more successful, or don't you?"

Shelley bit her bottom lip, feeling pulled in opposite directions. She remembered her promises to Missy, Anna, Miss Walters, and her mother, now that she'd earned her camp money.

Yet . . . her business was just getting exciting now. Her gaze wandered across the echoing Y gymnasium. Eager buyers swarmed from table to booth to display. Next year, she'd love a booth of her own at the flea market.

She lifted her chin and turned back to Jerome. "Yes, I definitely want my business to grow."

"Good! Then the next customer is yours." Jerome straightened a tilted lamp shade. "Remember: figure out what a customer wants, then give it to him. Naturally, you'll start with the most expensive items."

"All right." Shelley licked her lips and checked her straightened hair. "I'll try."

Five minutes later a young man in a beaded vest and frayed jeans approached the table. "Got any guitar music?" he drawled.

Shelley asked Jerome, who shook his head. "I'm sorry," she said. "We don't." She inspected the display for something else to interest him. Noting his beaded vest, she pointed to the Indian belt. "Um, you wouldn't want to buy this beaded belt, would you?"

"Don't wear belts." He pushed his long hair behind one ear and grinned. "See ya around." He started to shuffle away.

Jerome lunged forward. "Perhaps, since you're musically inclined, I might suggest this item." He held out a polished harmonica, complete with leather case.

"Well, I don't know," he said doubtfully.

Jerome put the harmonica in the man's hand. "Handy to take along on trips—just slip it into your pocket. Easier to carry than a guitar." He smiled at his small joke.

The young man blew softly into the harmonica. "I don't know how to play this thing though," he said.

"A simple instruction booklet is included, at no extra cost." Jerome held it out.

After glancing through the booklet and running his lips across the harmonica a few more times, the young man reached into his pocket. One at a time, he handed Jerome three dollar bills. He waved, then moved away, the soft breathy chords growing fainter.

"I'm sorry," Shelley said. "I almost blew a sale for you."

"No problem. You were just nervous." Jerome added the money to his gray change box. "Keep trying. I'll give you half the profit on anything you sell today."

"Really?" Shelley'd come to the flea market to learn about selling, but she'd never expected to make any money. "Thanks."

"That's okay. Incentive works wonders."

Shelley polished two pair of sunglasses, then added

them to the display. If Jerome was going to pay her, at least she could be useful. "Do you always have so much inventory? I can't afford to tie up this much money."

"No, I bought extra for this flea market." He re-filled his dish of business cards.

"You found all this neat stuff at garage sales?"

"Mostly. Of course, I visit sales the night before they officially start. Otherwise things are picked over. If the newspaper says a sale starts Saturday morning, go Friday night. You beat the crowds that way. People will always sell early."

"You sure bought a ton of junk—er, merchandise."

"It's a business risk. But I made good money at last year's flea market, and I wanted to have extra inventory on hand this time." He turned his back to the crowd and combed his hair quickly.

"Is that why you went to the Salvation Army Thrift Store?"

"Yes, I tried to locate some items there that sold well at last year's flea market."

Shelley started to ask another question, but stopped abruptly. Approaching their booth from across the aisle was Miss Walters.

Shelley waved. "Miss Walters! Hi!"

"Hello, Shelley. How's business today?"

"Great so far. I'm just helping out. This is Jerome Potter, a friend of mine." Jerome nodded politely, then stepped to the back of the booth. Shelley knew he was just pretending to count change. He was really leaving her on her own.

Miss Walters studied Jerome. "Your friend's name sounds familiar. I believe I bought something from him last year at the bazaar."

Shelley waved her hand over the table. "Is there something special you're looking for today?"

"No, just whatever catches my eye." She glanced around the gym. "There are so many new booths today. It's more crowded than last year."

Shelley watched Miss Walters pick up, turn over, then put down five different items. Remembering Jerome's advice, she tried to think of something Miss Walters might need.

Then her eye caught the set of three sun-catchers on the table. They were like the clown she had in her bedroom window, but each stained-glass ornament was something from nature: a monarch butterfly, a robin in a nest, and a daffodil.

Shelley held up the sparkling yellow and orange daffodil. "Wouldn't this look pretty in a south window at school?"

"That *is* lovely. Looks springy, don't you think?"

Shelley smiled and held her breath.

"Let's see, it's marked two dollars." Miss Walters reached into her purse and handed Shelley the money.

Shelley took a shaky breath, then blurted out, "You can buy all three for only five dollars." She bit her lip, afraid of sounding pushy.

"Well, they do make a nice set." Miss Walters held the other two sun-catchers up to the light. "Yes, I'll take them all." She handed Shelley three more dollars.

After wrapping each piece of glass in tissue paper, Shelley packed them in a small box. "Thanks, Miss Walters. They'll really brighten up the classroom."

Jerome joined Shelley as her customer strolled away. "Nice work," he said. "Those sun-catchers cost me fifty cents each. That's a profit of three-fifty, or one dollar seventy-five for your share."

"Thanks!" Shelley filled the vacant spot in the display with a gold piggy bank. "That wasn't so terrible after all."

The crowd increased, then dwindled, then swelled again at irregular intervals. Jerome seemed to know a lot of people. At the busiest times, both Shelley and Jerome waited on customers. Shelley's shaky confidence grew with each sale. One man even mentioned seeing her picture in the *Sentinel*.

After the last customer left, Jerome removed some money and locked the cash box. "Here. This is half the profit from what you sold this afternoon." He handed her a small sheet of paper with her sales neatly itemized. Folded within the paper was thirteen dollars.

"This much?" Shelley'd lost track of her sales.

"You earned it." Jerome began wrapping and repacking his merchandise in the cartons under the table.

Shelley glanced at her watch. 7:10. It couldn't be! But around the gym, other sellers were packing too. The gym doors were closed, and only a few stragglers remained at the booths.

In silence Shelley packed the unsold bracelets, necklaces, and glass ornaments. Now that she had a minute to catch her breath, she was exhausted. What an afternoon it had been! She'd learned so much.

When she and Jerome were finished, she asked, "Do you want some help carrying these boxes somewhere?"

"No, my dad's bringing the station wagon to pick me up." Jerome hesitated, then stuck his hands in his back pockets. "I'm glad you came. Maybe we could do this again sometime."

Shelley squeezed around the end of the bare table. "I'd like that." She raised her voice over the din of booths being knocked down. "Thanks, Jerome. I learned a lot."

Walking home, Shelley's legs ached from standing six hours. But even though she was worn out, she tingled with excitement. Even jogging had never left her feeling so good.

It was a feeling she definitely liked.

12 ⁑ Ridiculous Daze

A BOX FROM the top closet shelf fell on Shelley's head, then dumped its contents onto the hall floor. Rubbing her head, she surveyed the mess.

Shelley was hunting through her mom's sewing scraps. At the flea market the day before, Jerome's jewelry and glass items had looked impressive against black velvet. Shelley intended to display her ceramic figures and glass dishes against some dark material too.

"Shelley, hurry up! The fire's ready!" Her dad's voice boomed through the open bedroom window.

"Coming!"

Most Sunday afternoons, Shelley's family cooked their dinner outside. Today's menu was roasted hot dogs.

Scooping up the jumble of remnants on the floor, she sorted quickly. Most of the material was too brightly patterned to use. At the bottom of the heap, however, she found a navy blue piece, just right for future displays.

After working at the flea market, Shelley finally felt comfortable with selling. She'd developed a shrewd eye for a bargain, had learned to dress for success, and had built some regular customers at school and in her neighborhood.

And the profits! Thirteen whole dollars just for a few hours of selling. The sky was the limit, if she was willing to work.

In fact, Shelley reasoned, with summer vacation just around the corner, it would be dumb to go out of business. With school out she'd have plenty of time for friends and family, while still working at her swapping.

"Shelley!" Missy pounded up the stairs, dragging Raggedy Ann by one leg. "I cooked your hot dog, but you have to come now and eat. Come on!"

"I'm coming." Shelley picked up the blue material, stuffed the scraps into the sack, and threw it on the shelf. Suddenly hungry, she followed Missy downstairs and out to the backyard.

The bright sun made Shelley squint. Her mouth watered at the picnic table loaded with food: hot dogs, corn chips, potato salad, and fresh sliced strawberries. Her mom and dad waited at the table. Cassie, in her infant swing, dozed in the shade.

"Sorry I took so long." Shelley slid onto the picnic bench. "I was looking for something."

Her mom dished up strawberries. "That's okay. We're just glad you're here today. We've missed having you around lately."

Her dad piled his hot dog high with relish. "With your book project done and your camp money raised, you can finally relax. I'm glad."

Shelley smiled and grabbed the mustard. She didn't have the nerve to tell them her book project had to be done over. Bending over her hot dog, she concentrated on writing her name in mustard.

As Shelley filled up on hot dogs and potato salad, she gradually relaxed. All through their chocolate sundaes, she and her dad tried to out-do each other with terrible knock-knock jokes.

Later, in the middle of toasting her fourth marshmallow, the telephone rang. "I'll get it." Shelley swallowed the gooey marshmallow on the way into the house, then picked up the phone. "Hello?"

"Is this the Gordon residence?" a rather high voice asked.

"Yup."

"Is Shelley there?"

"Jerome? Is that you?"

He cleared his throat, making the phone line crackle. "Yes, it is. I just heard something about Ridiculous Daze I thought you might be interested in."

"Ridiculous Daze?" Shelley wondered how the town's annual summer sale day could interest her. "What about it?"

"Do you usually go?"

"Sure, everybody does."

One day during the summer, the downtown stores set tables full of sale items out on the sidewalks, while game booths and eating stands were set up on the courthouse square. Salespeople had to wear funny costumes. Shelley and Anna went to Ridiculous Daze together every year.

Jerome's next words rushed out breathlessly. "My dad's on the town council, and this morning he said Ridiculous Daze has been moved up to the last week in June. That way it won't conflict with Madison's Centennial celebration in August."

"Why are you so interested in the date for Ridiculous Daze?"

"Dad said the council approved my application for a booth on the square this year. I'll sell things, like at the flea market."

"That's nice, but you've lost me."

He paused and cleared his throat again. "How about running the booth together? We'd have twice the merchandise that way. We'd each keep the profits from our own sales."

Shelley sat down at the desk with a thud. What a chance! What a terrific chance!

"Shelley? What do you think? It's six weeks away. We'd have plenty of time to stock up on less expensive items. People don't expect to spend a lot of money on Ridiculous Daze."

Shelley took a deep breath. "If you're sure, I'd

really like to. I'll get busy right away and find less expensive things to sell."

"Do you have to ask your parents?"

"I'll ask, but I know they'll say okay. It won't interfere with school work or anything." Her mind skipped back and forth, making a mental list of items to look for.

"I'll check back with you in a week or two. What about wearing matching costumes? If they were unusual enough, we might get our picture in the paper. Free advertising, you know."

"Of course." Shelley needed to train herself to think "business" like Jerome did. "Thanks for asking me. What day is it again?"

"Last Friday in June. The twenty-ninth."

"I'll circle it on the calendar and get busy right away." Hanging up, Shelley waltzed around the kitchen, waving her marshmallow stick like a magic wand.

Back at the desk she grabbed a red felt marker and flipped the calendar page to June. She'd circle the date right away. Bending over eagerly, she stopped short.

A bold black line was drawn through the last week of June. In her mom's square printed letters were the words "Shelley—Forest Lake."

Shelley stared at the words until they blurred. How could she have forgotten the camp dates? On June 29 she'd still be at Forest Lake. Right after school the next day she and Anna were going to register.

Slumped at the desk, Shelley snapped her stick in two. *Why* did Jerome's offer have to come at the same time as camp?

She leaned back, balancing the wooden chair on two legs. Jerome's idea was so tempting! However, she couldn't share his booth unless she stayed home. If she cancelled her plans for camp, though, would Anna ever speak to her again?

She paced circles around the tiny kitchen. Maybe she was making a mountain out of a molehill. Anna was already twelve. She'd get along fine at camp without her. Lots of girls from other summers would be back, so Anna'd still have fun.

Running sticky fingers through her hair, Shelley was surprised at her feelings. She'd worked so hard to be able to go to camp. But if she had to choose between Forest Lake with Anna and Ridiculous Daze with Jerome, she'd take sharing Jerome's booth. She didn't dare pass up this big chance.

Shelley finally wandered back outside. She dropped her marshmallow stick onto the coals.

"Who was on the phone?" her mom asked, rewinding Cassie's baby swing.

"Jerome Potter. He asked me to share a booth with him. This time I'd be selling my own things."

"When?" Her father poured water over the crumbling white coals.

"On Ridiculous Daze. He gets to have a booth on

the square." She stacked dirty paper plates and styrofoam cups.

"Tom, what do you think?" Her mother adjusted the swing to shade Cassie's face.

Her dad stirred the doused fire. "I don't see why not. Shelley should have plenty of time during the summer, without the pressure of schoolwork."

"Thanks, Dad." Shelley was relieved her parents had agreed so quickly. But as she washed the plastic silverware to save for the next picnic, worry about disappointing Anna nagged at the back of her mind.

Maybe she was just borrowing trouble. If she changed her mind about camp, would Anna really be so upset? She hardly ever got mad. Shelley nodded firmly, convinced it would take something a lot worse than missing camp to affect their friendship.

Shelley shook out the checked table cloth while remembering past summers at Forest Lake. She loved the trail hikes, the singalongs around evening campfires, the afternoon swims. Did she want to give that up, after she'd worked so hard to earn the forty-five dollars? Was having a booth at Ridiculous Daze so important?

Maybe it shouldn't be, Shelley admitted, but it was.

On Ridiculous Daze she'd have customers from the entire town of Madison, not just her neighbors or the kids at school. After her experience at the flea market, she was confident she could handle it.

And all that money! If she could make thirteen dollars splitting a few hours' profits, she should rake in three times that amount when she could keep it all. She'd be rich in just one day! She'd have a ball spending all that money.

After putting the table cloth away, Shelley took their Sears catalog up to her bedroom. With it open on her lap, she turned the pages slowly. The colorful collection of clothes, record albums, and jewelry could be hers someday!

By skipping camp she'd save the forty-five dollars. Added to what she earned during the summer, she'd have enough to buy anything she wanted. She'd get some things for her family too—she wanted to be generous. But tons of money would be left over to spend however she wished.

She flipped through the catalog for an hour and her dreams grew with each page. In the bathing suit section, Shelley spotted a petite model who reminded her of Anna. Feeling guilty again, she closed the catalog.

"Face it," she told herself sternly. "There's one giant, humongous problem to solve first." She had to tell Anna she'd changed her mind about camp.

Shelley decided to get it over with. Her heart thudding, she tried three different times to call Anna. Each time the phone rang and rang, until nine o'clock when Shelley finally quit trying. She'd have to talk to Anna first thing in the morning. She hoped Anna took the news as well as her parents had.

Earlier that evening when she'd explained about camp, they'd listened quietly. Burping Cassie gently, her mother finally spoke. "Are you sure about this?" She'd sounded doubtful.

Her dad, however, was very matter-of-fact. "It's your decision, Shelley. You earned that money. If you'd rather save it than go to camp, it's up to you."

Shelley'd been relieved. That was one great thing about her parents. When possible, they let her make her own decisions—without trying to make her feel guilty.

If only Anna would react the same way.

The next morning Shelley arrived at school fifteen minutes early. As soon as she spotted Anna a block away, she hurried to meet her.

"Hi!" Anna shouted, running to meet her. "Can you believe it? We finally get to sign up for camp today! How was your weekend?"

"Fine." Shelley paused, unsure now how to begin. "I worked with Jerome at the flea market Saturday," she said slowly. "It was a lot of fun and—"

"I had fun Saturday too. Guess what? I finally found enough cups and matching saucers for my candle party." She flung her dark braids over her shoulder. "I want to invite everyone for Friday night. As soon as I clear it with Mom, that is."

"Candle party?"

"You know. At the party everyone's going to make a candle in a cup to take home."

"Oh, yeah." Shelley took a deep breath. "I want to talk—"

"Me, too, about Forest Lake! That's all I've

thought about since you earned enough money to go. I always knew you'd make it."

Shelley groaned inwardly. Anna was making it hard. She'd just have to blurt it out.

"I've thought a lot about camp too. Something's come up, though. I don't think I'll be going." *There, she'd said it.*

The hurt expression on Anna's face made Shelley's stomach turn over. Staring at the sidewalk, Shelley wished she were no bigger than the red ladybug that crawled in the crack. The morning sun warmed the back of her neck while the silence dragged out.

"What's come up?" Anna finally asked in a small voice.

"Jerome called yesterday. Until then, I *had* intended to register for camp this afternoon."

"Jerome Potter? What's he got to do with Forest Lake?"

"He's having a booth on Ridiculous Daze. He asked me to bring my merchandise and share the booth."

"But that's not till August."

"Not this year. It interfered with the centennial stuff planned in August. Ridiculous Daze was moved to the last Friday in June." Shelley's voice trailed off uncertainly.

"Oh."

Anna stood perfectly still and stared at her. No sniffling, no big sighs. Just silence.

Shelley touched Anna's arm. "We'll go lots of

places together this summer. Since I'll have more money, we won't have to miss a single carnival or county fair or good movie that comes to the Orpheum."

"Sure." Anna shifted her books to her other arm. "I guess I can go to camp alone. It won't be the same without you, though."

"I wouldn't blame you for being mad."

"I'm not mad." Anna played with the end of her braid, yanking out individual hairs. "We'll do stuff when you're not busy. It's okay."

Shelley finally began to relax. Maybe it *was* going to be all right.

She never should have doubted Anna—they'd been best friends for five years. Not going to camp together one summer wouldn't change anything. Side by side, they walked into school together.

The rest of the week Shelley had little time to worry about Anna. Working several hours each evening, she finally finished *Sensible Kate* and *Sarah's Idea* by Thursday.

She propped her new chart on the desk Thursday night and rewrote her paper from the careful notes she'd taken. At eleven o'clock she tried to flex the writer's cramp out of her fingers. The project paper was done, and this time she knew it was good.

Friday morning she turned in her project paper. That evening she felt pounds lighter as she pedaled down High Street to "preview" four Saturday garage sales. On Jerome's advice, she was visiting the sales the night before they officially started. She kicked herself for not thinking of it on her own.

Jerome was right, no doubt about it. She covered the sales in record time. There were no shoving crowds to fight, and none of the merchandise was picked over. It was nearly seven o'clock when she headed home. She counted sixteen new items in her bike basket as she pedaled lazily down Lexington Avenue.

As she turned the corner onto Jefferson, she braked and coasted to a halt. Charlene minced across the street directly in front of her.

"Hi, Charlene," Shelley called, balancing on one foot.

"Hi. What are you doing?" Charlene crossed her arms and jutted out one hip of her designer jeans.

"Hunting things for my swap box." Shelley wheeled the bike to the curb. On the spur of the moment, she asked, "Want to call Anna and Kendra and go out to the shopping center?"

Shelley felt like celebrating, even with Charlene. No school for two more days, and she'd finally finished her book project. Again.

"I don't have time." Charlene brushed invisible dust from her suede shoes. "I'm already late."

"For what?"

Charlene's innocent eyes opened wide. "Anna's candle-making party, of course."

Shelley frowned. Anna was having her party *tonight*? Since Monday morning, Anna hadn't mentioned it again. Until that minute, Shelley'd forgotten all about it.

She wanted to smack Charlene's smug face. "Have a good time," she said through gritted teeth.

"Sorry you weren't invited. Anna didn't ask you because she knew you'd be too busy to come." Charlene shrugged her shoulders.

"Yeah."

Pretending not to care, Shelley wheeled on down the street. She couldn't believe it! Anna, her very best friend in the world, was having a party and hadn't invited her.

Loose gravel near the gutter made Shelley skid sharply. Catching herself, she decided to walk her bike for a while. She needed some time to think before she reached home. Scuffing along the sidewalk, she was barely aware of the blocks she covered.

She thought about Anna's behavior during the past week. When Anna had registered for camp Monday, Shelley'd been relieved. They hadn't discussed camp again all week. Shelley'd turned her attention to rewriting her book project.

Rubbing her throbbing temples, Shelley wondered if she'd expected her best friend to understand too much. Or maybe their friendship was fading after spending so little time together. Whatever the reason, Shelley knew by the churning in her stomach that something had gone terribly wrong.

13  Too Late

SHELLEY MOANED as she struggled out of bed Saturday morning. She ached all over, just like when she'd come down with the flu in January. Dragging herself to the mirror, she stuck out her tongue and peered closely.

Everything looked normal. No white spots. No swollen red throat. Just a bitter-tasting white coating on her tongue. She wrinkled her nose at the taste.

Downstairs, Shelley trudged into the sunny kitchen and frowned at the radio's blare. Some country western singer was advertising used cars with an ear-splitting jingle. Her mom and dad relaxed at the newly finished oak table, absorbed in different sections of the morning paper.

"Hi, Sleepyhead." Her mom folded the paper. "Want a waffle? I kept some warm."

"No, thanks. I'm not hungry."

At the kitchen window Shelley pulled back the gingham curtains. A blur caught her eye. She watched as Corduroy chased monarch butterflies around the backyard. She sighed and let the curtain drop. Where did that dog get so much energy?

"You feeling all right?" her mom asked as she snapped off the radio. "You look pale. Maybe you're running a temp." She pushed her hand under Shelley's bangs to test for fever.

"I'm just tired, that's all," Shelley mumbled.

She couldn't explain the real reason her stomach churned. How did you say that your best friend had dumped you? Especially if it was your own fault.

Her dad looked up from the sports page. "It's no wonder you're exhausted. You've driven yourself too hard lately. Can't you just skip the garage sales today and take it easy?"

Shelley rummaged in the refrigerator for a ripe pear. "Probably not. With Ridiculous Daze next month, I shouldn't take a chance on missing a good bargain." She tried to force some enthusiasm into her voice.

Her dad refolded the *Sentinel*. "Sure you're not regretting your decision to skip camp?"

Shelley slumped into a chair. "No, I'm just pooped. Maybe I *could* take it easy today. I hit the biggest garage sales last night anyway."

Licking the pear juice that ran down her arm, Shelley decided that maybe her dad was right about easing off a little. In fact, she knew exactly what she'd love to do that morning.

Upstairs she pulled on her most faded cut-offs and "I Love My Dog" T-shirt. She didn't even bother to comb her wild mop of unironed curls before padding back downstairs and outside.

The cool air was filled with the delicate scent of the lilacs that bloomed beside the garage. Shelley stood on the back step for a moment, stretched up on tiptoe, and breathed deeply.

"I can't believe it. I really have some free time," she thought. She wanted to lie in the grass, feel the sun on her face, and hold a dozing Corduroy in her lap while she stroked his silky ears.

Surely, in such a peaceful setting, she could think clearly and figure out where her plans had fallen apart. Shelley headed around the corner of the house.

"Here, Corduroy! Here, boy!"

Shelley sat crosslegged in the grass, the newly mown stubble tickling the backs of her thighs. At her whistle, Corduroy bounded toward her.

Forty pounds of muscle and fur landed on top of her, and Shelley was knocked over backward. Exasperated, she shoved at the drooling dog.

"Corduroy! Get off me!" Pushing him aside, she struggled to sit up again. Her head already ached. Banging it on the hard ground hadn't helped any. "Now, come here, boy. Calm down and lie here on my lap. Come *on*."

Instead, Corduroy darted to his doghouse. In ten

seconds, he raced back and dropped his chewed ball in her lap. Saliva dripped from his tongue as he licked Shelley's face up and down.

"Gross! Corduroy, stop spitting on me!" She wiped her face with her shirt tail. "Come on, boy, just lie down beside me." She reached out to stroke his back, but he was off and running again.

He circled around her, just out of her reach, as if playing a game. Corduroy bounded up, then fell to the ground, rolled over, and leaped up again. Dodging behind Shelley, he jumped up on her back, his wet nose nuzzling her hair.

Shelley jerked around, her arm flying. "Oh, bug off, Corduroy!"

Ashamed of her sharp tone of voice, she glanced at the house. She hoped no one had overheard her. After all, Corduroy just wanted to play.

She grumbled as she stomped back to the house. All she'd wanted was a little peace and quiet, some time to think. She *was* glad Corduroy was excited to see her, but at that moment, she just wanted him to go away and leave her alone.

Sneaking around the house, Shelley used the front door. No one noticed her come in there. Inside, the sound of singing chipmunks on TV drowned out her footsteps as she crept upstairs. With any luck, she'd avoid her entire family.

In her room Shelley locked the door and paced to the window and back. Tense and keyed up, she bent and snapped out twenty toe-touches and leg-lunges.

It didn't help.

She couldn't pinpoint exactly when her life had gotten out of control, but she hated the feeling. No matter how often her overtired mind wandered off, it always returned to the same point. *Anna.*

Anna, her best friend. Or was she? Shelley wasn't sure anymore.

Spotting her jogging shoes halfway under the bed gave Shelley an idea. In a spurt of energy, she pulled them on, then headed back downstairs. In the past she'd done her clearest thinking while jogging.

She covered the first block easily. During the second block, she gasped slightly. By the third block, she was forced to slow down. The painful stitch in her side reminded her how often she'd skipped her morning run lately.

At the end of eight blocks, she admitted defeat. Her knotted calf muscles forced her to give in and walk the rest of the way.

Although her legs and rib cage ached, Shelley felt more relaxed than she had in weeks. Leaning against a tree at the edge of Baybridge Park, she gazed up at the fluttering oak leaves and blue sky beyond.

Just as she'd hoped, running had cleared her head of the cobwebs. *Put first things first.* Hobbling along Jefferson Street, her choice was finally clear.

Back home, Shelley picked up the phone before she lost her nerve. She was convinced she'd made the right decision, but it still wasn't easy.

"Jerome? I'm sorry, but something important's

come up. I can't share your booth on Ridiculous Daze after all." She paused and listened. "No, it was okay with my parents. This is my own decision. Thanks for asking me though. Maybe next year."

The dial tone hummed in her ear for a moment before she hung up. Turning, she saw her dad leaning against the doorway. Shrugging, Shelley wiped her sweaty hands on her shorts.

"You changed your mind about camp?" he asked quietly.

Shelley sank into a kitchen chair. "I thought about what you said. You were right. I was giving up too much."

Her father joined her at the table. "I know you'll miss being part of Jerome's booth. Have you told Anna yet?"

"No, I'll call Mr. Jackson first and register. We'd planned to sign up as soon as I earned the forty-five dollars. Anna registered last Monday, but there's still two days left before the deadline."

"I think you'll be glad you changed your mind." He patted her hand lightly. "I know Anna will be pleased."

Shelley brightened at his words. She couldn't wait to see the expression on Anna's face when she told her. Right after calling Mr. Jackson, she'd bike over and break the news in person.

"I'll call right now." Shelley reached for the phone. "Mr. Jackson? This is Shelley Gordon. I want to sign up for the junior high cabin at Forest Lake. I can bring the registration money over this afternoon.''

The camp director's voice crackled through the bad connection. "I'm sorry, Shelley, but there isn't any more room. We filled up last Wednesday.''

"I thought the deadline wasn't until the thirtieth!''

"Officially that *is* the deadline, but the turnout was much greater this spring. We filled our cabin quotas early. I'm terribly sorry.''

Shelley slowly slid down the side of the refrigerator to sit on the floor. "You couldn't squeeze in just one more person?'' she pleaded.

"Not unless someone cancels. There are only so many bunks.'' He paused, then added, "I'll take down your name. Then, if someone cancels, I'll notify you first. I'm afraid that's the best I can do.''

Shelley twisted the phone cord. "I understand. Thanks anyway.'' She hung up, then turned to her dad. "There's no more room.''

"So I gathered.'' He took two Jonathan apples from the fruit bowl on the table and tossed one to Shelley. "Come outside with me while I water the garden.''

Feet dragging, Shelley followed her dad outside. As she sat glumly beside the garden, Shelley barely noticed when Corduroy bounded by and swiped her apple.

Her dad unwound the rubber hose and stretched it from the house to the garden. Turning the faucet on full force made the green hose wiggle like a snake.

Her dad didn't talk until all the tomato, pepper, and cauliflower plants had been thoroughly soaked. Turning off the faucet, he came and squatted beside her.

"What made you change your mind about camp?"

Shelley pulled up a blade of grass, bit off the tender white root, then shredded the blade. "Last night Anna had a party, and I wasn't even invited. Charlene said Anna knew I was too busy to come."

"That must have hurt."

"It did. A lot." Shelley tossed the bits of grass over her shoulder. "Anna doesn't act mad at me or anything. We just aren't best friends anymore."

"I see. To show Anna you still want to be best friends, you decided to go to camp after all?"

Shelley nodded. "But the junior high cabin is already full. I'd feel too stupid to call Jerome and change my mind again, so I lost out both ways."

"I think you were right to try to fix things when you decided you'd made a mistake." Her dad rubbed his whiskers. The scratching sounded like sandpaper. "Unfortunately, sometimes the opportunity is gone."

"Then what should I do? Everything's such a mess."

"It's true that you can't go to Forest Lake with Anna, but you could plan something else. Something special for the two of you."

"Like what?" Nothing would make up for missing camp. "You know Madison's a dud town. There's nothing to do here."

"Well then, what about the water slide in Thornton?

I could take you at one when it opens and pick you up when the park closes at eight. Of course, you'd have to go on a Saturday when I don't work."

Shelley leaned back on her elbows. "Wet and Wild *is* a lot of fun. Besides the water slides, there's lots of neat souvenir shops and tons of eating places. I could pay Anna's admission and my own. My treat."

"When would you like to go?"

Thoughtfully, Shelley pulled up a handful of grass. "We could go the Saturday after school's out. Kind of a getting out of school celebration."

"Fine with me."

Her dad tossed a chewed rubber ball into Shelley's lap, and Corduroy landed on her trying to retrieve it. Falling over backwards, Shelley laughed hard for the first time in weeks.

An hour later Shelley dialed Anna's number. She avoided mentioning the candle party the night before. Pretending nothing was wrong, she outlined her plan. Anna sounded surprised at Shelley's invitation, but really pleased.

After Shelley hung up, she jumped high into the air and landed with a crash. Cassie, who lay chewing on the table leg, jerked around and let out a startled wail. Patting her baby sister's thickly diapered bottom, Shelley decided things might work out after all.

14 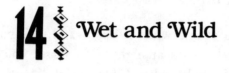 Wet and Wild

O N MONDAY MORNING Shelley was amazed to find Jon Kruger lounging on top of her desk when she arrived at school. As usual, his super looks took her breath away.

"Hi, Jon." Shelley ducked in embarrassment at the sound of her quivering voice.

"Hi, Shelley. Just the girl I wanted to see." Jon slid from her desk and stepped back so she could sit down.

"Me? What for?" Shelley smoothed her hair, glad she'd asked her mom to iron it that morning.

"Those South Seas decorations were so neat that I decided to ask you for another favor. I'm having a party, and I could use your help."

Shelley gazed into Jon's dark brown eyes, then

tore her glance away. With him so close, she couldn't think clearly.

"What kind of help?" she finally croaked out.

"I'm having a Western-type party. You know, a barbecue, a huge bonfire, and a hayride." He smiled at Miss Walters when she cleared her throat and stared at him. "How about helping me with the decorations?"

Shelley relaxed a little. Now he was talking about something she understood. "What did you have in mind?"

"Oh, maybe little cowboys and Indians to decorate the tables. Or horse models. I'm going to tell everybody to come in costume, but it wouldn't hurt if I had some old cowboy hats or Indian headbands for people who can't find a costume."

Shelley scribbled his ideas on a sheet of notebook paper. The party sounded like fun, she thought wistfully.

"How about strings of tiny beads for the Indians?" She chewed on her pencil eraser. "Or a kid's sheriff costume if I can find one, with a badge or gun and holster."

"Great!" Jon winked at her. "Of course you're invited."

Shelley's hand jerked, breaking her pencil lead. "I am? Thanks." She tossed her useless pencil into her desk. "I'd love to come."

"About the payment—Mom gave me ten dollars

to spend for decorations." He pulled an envelope from his jeans pocket and handed it to Shelley. "The party's in three weeks. Maybe you could come out to our farm and help me decorate the afternoon of the party."

"Maybe." Shelley couldn't imagine anything she'd enjoy more.

The whole party sounded like a dream. Or a movie. A soft starry night. Singing songs around a glowing campfire. The soft strumming of a guitar. Jon in a cowboy hat . . . It sounded so romantic. And Jon wanted *her* to come!

Miss Walters scowled slightly, then rapped her ruler on the corner of her desk.

"Got to go." Jon stood and stretched. "By the way, the date's June eighth." With a smile and a wave, he headed across the room.

Shelley's smile froze. Her heart beat so hard it hurt. *June eighth?* It couldn't be!

All year she'd prayed Jon would notice her. At last he had. But June eighth! That was the day after school got out—the date she'd invited Anna to go to the Wet and Wild Water Slide.

All morning Shelley barely heard a word Miss Walters said. She spent her time doing two things: *one*, staring at the back of Jon's head, and *two*, wondering how she could manage to go to his party without hurting Anna's feelings again. There *had* to be a way. She'd been waiting eight months for Jon Kruger to discover her.

When the noon bell rang, she still didn't know what to do.

Anna zipped across the room. "Ready?" She waved her green lunch ticket in Shelley's face. "Hurry up. It's tacos and doughnuts today."

All through lunch, Anna chattered about her piano recital coming up. Shelley only half-listened, her mind still on her problem. The obvious solution was to ask Anna to go to the water slides another time. She'd understand. Probably.

Shelley rolled the shredded cheese from her taco into little greasy balls. From biggest to smallest, she lined them up on her plate.

Maybe there was another answer, she thought. Should she tell Jon she was tied up that day? Maybe he'd change the date of the party so she could come. Even as that thought crossed her mind, Shelley figured it was one chance in a million. If she weren't providing the decorations, she suspected she wouldn't have been invited anyway.

"—and I'll wear my new navy-and-white striped suit."

"What?" Shelley blinked several times and took a bite out of the cold taco in her hand. "I didn't hear you."

"I said I'd wear my new swimming suit the day we go to Wet and Wild. You'll love it." Anna crunched into her second taco, spraying lettuce and cheese across the table. "I can't wait to go. Less than three weeks away!"

Shelley nodded miserably. Now was the time to tell Anna about Jon's party. "That reminds me—" But as she watched her best friend, she knew she couldn't do it.

She'd already canceled so many plans with Anna. On her list of priorities, Anna's friendship should rank higher than Jon's party.

She could still sell Jon the decorations. If he honestly liked her, he'd invite her to other parties. Even so, she hated to miss that one.

Anna snapped her fingers in front of Shelley's face. "Hey! Yoo-hoo. What did you start to say?"

"Oh, just that Dad said we could stay until the park closed at eight. What shows and shops do you want to go to?"

Anna tore her glazed doughnut into four equal pieces. "I love the Mermaid Market with all the souvenirs made from shells. I thought I'd buy a huge shell and fill it with colored wax for a giant candle."

"Sounds neat." Shelley sighed as she glimpsed Jon seated across the cafeteria with Lisa. Deliberately turning back to Anna, she asked, "Want to eat lunch at the Seaweed Shop this time?"

"Sure, plus tons of snacks in between." Anna licked her sugary fingers. "This will be a great way to celebrate getting out of school."

Shelley poked at her taco. Orange grease ran down her fingers when she tore off a bite of shell. Humming "Home on the Range" under her breath, she added her soggy taco to the lump already in her stomach.

The next weeks rushed by, with end-of-the-school-year work to finish. Although Shelley told Jon she couldn't make it to his western party, she spent every spare minute hunting for decorations.

By the last day of school, she had an impressive collection. Besides checking the garage sales, she'd taken Jerome's advice about the Thrift Store. The sales lady recognized Shelley from the newspaper picture and agreed to watch for certain items for her.

As a result, Shelley'd been able to buy two full cowboy and Indian Halloween costumes, an Indian drum, and a string of authentic-looking rubber bear claws for some "Indian" to wear around his neck. Added to what Jon had asked her to find, she had two cardboard boxes full of decorations.

On the last day of classes Shelley's dad gave her a lift to school. Together they carried the boxes of decorations into her classroom. Shelley motioned for Jon to follow her to the back of the room.

While Miss Walters wrote division problems on the blackboard, Shelley laid the items out on an empty table for Jon to inspect. When she pulled out the drum and bear teeth, Jon was just as impressed as Shelley'd hoped he be.

Then she repacked the decorations. "I'm glad you like everything. I hope your party is a lot of fun."

"Thanks. I'm sorry you can't come." He taped the box lids shut. "Say, do you go to Ridiculous Daze?"

"Sure. This year it's the last Friday in June." Her heart beat wildly, wondering what he was leading up to.

"I always go too." He hoisted both boxes into his arms. "Maybe I'll see you there." He turned to go, giving her a slow wink.

"You never know." Shelley half-smiled, disappointed he hadn't said anything more definite. And yet, he *had* asked if she'd be there.

But would she be?

She hoped so, but Jon might not recognize her in costume. While working hard for Jon's party the past two weeks, she'd decided it was silly not to call Jerome back. Swapping was fun, and she wanted to build her business. The previous evening she'd swallowed her pride and told Jerome she could come after all.

The dismissal bell echoed down the school corridors. A whooping yell went up from the entire class. Miss Walters grinned and covered her ears, then finished distributing report cards in their manilla envelopes.

Shelley's grocery sack overflowed with junk from her now empty desk. With the sack balanced on her hip, she laid her folded report card on top. The B-minus in English had left her limp with relief.

Waving to Anna, she called, "Lets get out of here."

"I'm coming." Anna slammed her desk lid, grabbed her overstuffed book bag, and followed Shelley outside. "Just think," she said, wiping her sweaty face, "tomorrow at this very minute we'll be landing in pools of crystal clear cold water."

"*Ahhhhhhhhh,*" Shelley breathed. "I can't wait." With school finally out and the work for Jon finished, a day just for fun sounded like heaven.

Shelley and Anna arrived at the Wet and Wild Water Slide Park just before one o'clock. The day was a scorcher, but perfect weather for getting dunked. For two solid hours, they raced, laughing and soaked, from one slippery slide to another.

Some slides curved gently, like the Seahorse Slide meant for small kids. Giggling, Shelley and Anna coasted down its easy slope among herds of pre-schoolers. However, their terrified screams on the way down the giant Coral Corkscrew were real.

Exhaustion set in at three-thirty. "Let's take a break," Anna begged, dizzy after their last ride.

Wearing their terry cloth cover-ups and rubber thongs, they headed for the row of snack bars. After huge strawberry slushes, Shelley and Anna hunted through the overpriced souvenir shops. The searing sun baked their skin and dried their hair.

Emerging from a shop, Shelley blinked at the bright sun. "Where to now?"

"I'm hungry again. Want to get some hot dogs? Let me see how much money I—" Anna stopped abruptly and whirled around. "Oh, no!"

"What's the matter?"

"I left my billfold in the souvenir shop. I'll be right back." She rushed into the small store, her thongs slapping the sidewalk.

Anna vanished through the glass door, her black braids reminding Shelley of an Indian princess. Her own hairdo contrasted sharply in the window's reflection.

Her red hair, dried by the scorching sun, had long since lost its ironed look. She'd forgotten her barrettes, so her curls tumbled haphazardly around her face.

Taking off her sunglasses, Shelley shook her frizzy hair. No doubt about it—she'd left her "dress for success" look at home. No one would rush up to her at the water slide that afternoon and ask, "Aren't you the business tycoon we read about in the *Sentinel?*"

And she didn't care.

Oh, she wasn't fooling herself. She knew her swapping business was very important to her. But there was a time for everything: a time for work, and a time for friends.

She saluted as Anna reappeared in front of the shop.

"Got it." Anna waved her wallet in the air. "Let's eat!"

"I'm right behind you." Shelley linked her arm through Anna's, did a smooth about-face, and headed for a foot-long hot dog to share.